BOUND BY THE GLASS SLIPPER

SHORT, DARK, CINDERELLA RETELLING ROMANCE

FAE RINGS
BOOK TWO

JAX WILDER

Published by Rainbow Quartz Publishing

RQPublishing.com

RainbowQuartzPublishing@gmail.com

Edmonds, WA 98026

ISBN:978-1-961714-66-3

Cover design by Miranda Townsend

Edited by Miranda Townsend

First Edition: December 2024

CHAPTER 1
HER

The moment I saw them together—kissing—something inside me shattered.

It wasn't just the betrayal or the shock; it was the realization that everything I thought was stable had been an illusion all along.

"Mark, how could you?"

The words slipped out before I could catch them, raw and tinged with desperation.

He spun around, his expression shifting from surprise to guilt in a blink.

Beside him, she—his coworker Jenna—looked equally mortified, clutching her purse like it could shield her from the fallout.

"Ember, I—" Mark started, stepping toward me.

I raised my hand, stopping him mid-stride.

"Don't."

The word came out sharper than I expected, echoing off the walls of the empty street. "Don't say anything. I've seen enough."

Mark hesitated, one foot still angled toward me, as if that might change something. His lips parted, like he had a script to read from, and Jenna shrank behind him like a coward with a Coach bag.

"Ember, it's not—" he started.

"Not what?" I snapped, my voice rising. "Not what it looks like? You had your tongue in her mouth, Mark."

His expression twisted—caught between a grimace and a smirk, like he couldn't quite decide whether to beg or gaslight. "I mean... yeah, okay. But we never exactly *defined* things."

I blinked. Laughed once. Dark and sharp and bitter. "Excuse me?"

"I just mean—we never made it, like, *exclusive-exclusive*. You know I don't like labels."

"Oh my fucking God," I said, nearly choking on the words. "We've been together for two and a half years. I practically lived at your place. I did your laundry. I met your mother, Mark."

He shrugged, like that meant nothing. "Yeah, but you knew where I stood. I've always said I needed space. Freedom. I thought we had an understanding."

"You mean *you* had an understanding, and I had a fantasy you let me live in?" I could feel the heat rising up my neck now, my pulse pounding like a war drum. "Is that what this was to you? Me cooking you dinner, rubbing your back, pretending to come during five minutes of limp humping? That was just me playing house in my head?"

"Don't be dramatic."

"Don't be a fucking coward."

Jenna made some kind of soft noise, like she wanted to vanish into the pavement. Mark put a hand up, still trying to de-escalate the mess he created. "It was a kiss, Ember. That's it. It didn't mean anything."

"Neither did the dating apps you were scrolling on while I slept, right?"

His face went pale, then red. "That was—That's not what you think—"

"Oh? Then give me your phone."

I held out my hand, palm up. "Let's see what I *think*."

He didn't move.

"That's what I thought."

I dropped my hand, disgust curling in my chest like bile. "I let it go when I caught you the first time. I let it go when you told me I was too sensitive, or 'imagining things.' When you said Jenna was *just a friend*, even though you were texting her at midnight while I was crying in the goddamn shower."

Mark looked around nervously, like someone might walk by and witness his ego implode.

"I let it go when you told me I should be flattered that you *still wanted me*, even though I 'wasn't as hot as I used to be.' Remember that? Or how about the time you told me my laugh was annoying in front of your friends?"

"Ember—"

"No. You don't get to call me that. Not like it means something. Not after this."

His hand twitched at his side like he was about to reach for me, but even he must've known that bridge was on fire.

"I'm sorry," he said again, weaker this time. "It didn't mean anything. You mean something. Please don't walk away like this."

I tilted my head and gave him a look that could cut glass. "I faked every orgasm for two years, Mark. You *do* have a small dick. The only thing you ever satisfied was your own ego."

Jenna winced. I hoped it hurt.

He opened his mouth—maybe to defend his honor, maybe to throw another excuse into the void —but I was done.

"We're done," I said. Calm. Cold. Finished. "I hope she's worth it."

I turned and walked away, and I didn't look back.

Let the metaphorical door slam shut behind me.

Let him rot in the ashes.

My heart pounded in my chest, broken—but lighter than it had felt in months.

Hurt. Furious.

And finally, free.

As I MOVED DOWN the street, away from the wreckage of my so-called happy relationship, I needed something—anything—to erase the pain.

That's when I saw Lilly Drake's.

The mystical little shop I'd always passed but never entered. It promised secrets. Escapes. Magic.

And tonight, I was ready to believe in all three.

I pushed open the old wooden door. A brass bell tinkled overhead, greeting me like an old friend.

The air inside was cool and lavender-scented, with a mossy undercurrent that made it feel like I'd stepped into a forest instead of a shop.

Lilly Drake isn't like any jewelry store I've ever been to.

Here, the ordinary rules of retail don't apply.

Shelves and tables act more like altars—each one displaying trinkets that seem to hum with hidden purpose.

Glass orbs with swirling mists.

Necklaces that shimmer without light.

Rings that whisper to your bones, if you listen close enough.

But today, I wasn't here to window-shop.

I wasn't looking for sparkle. I was looking for something real.

As I turned a corner, a ring caught my eye.

Simple. Silver. Unassuming.

The band was bare save for a single, uncut stone —dark and oddly magnetic.

I leaned closer. Within its depths, tiny flecks of light danced like distant stars trapped in a night sky.

"Beautiful, isn't it?"

I jumped slightly, startled by the soft voice beside me.

Rainbow Rivers, the shopkeeper, stood nearby, wearing a smile that knew too much. Her voice was gentle—like the breeze that rolls in just after sunset.

She looked me over, warm but sharp-eyed. Like she could see past the mask I'd barely managed to hold together.

"Seems like you're carrying some heavy thoughts today, Ember." She folded her hands.

"Sometimes things fall away so that better things can find us. You were right to leave what no longer serves you. If you ask me, he wasn't worth your time."

I blinked. Caught between surprise and amusement.

"You got all that from a glance?" I asked, trying to mask my vulnerability with a laugh.

Rainbow's smile deepened. "When you work with magic, you learn to see beneath the surface."

Her eyes twinkled. "And my dear, the universe has plans far beyond anyone with a two-inch... well, you know."

I laughed—louder than I meant to. "Two inches would be generous. You're being way too kind," I snorted.

"I could've left him months ago, but I guess I was blinded. By the charm. Or maybe just by the routine."

"Then it's time for something new," Rainbow said, still gentle. "The right things show up when we're ready to see them."

I turned back to the ring.

It wasn't loud or flashy. It was quiet, waiting.

Mysterious. Like it had secrets meant only for me.

My fingers hovered over the metal.

A strange calm washed over me. Maybe... just maybe, I was exactly where I needed to be.

"This is... mesmerizing," I breathed. "It feels like it's calling to me."

Rainbow nodded. Her gaze sparkled. "It's said the ring chooses its wearer, not the other way around. It appears to those searching for something more—something beyond what they've dared to imagine."

My hand hovered, drawn by something I couldn't name.

"And what is it I'm searching for?" I asked, half-joking. Half-desperate.

"That's for you to answer," she said, lowering her voice to a whisper. "But be warned. The journey it offers has a cost. The ring will take you where you belong... but returning? That's never as simple as leaving."

A shiver ran through me—equal parts fear and fascination.

I wanted to ask more.

But the pull was too strong.

My fingers closed around the cool metal, and in that moment, it felt inevitable.

"I'll take it," I whispered. My voice felt small, but sure.

Rainbow studied me with eyes full of ancient knowing. Then she nodded. "Very well."

She wrapped the ring in soft cloth and placed it in my hand.

"Remember, it's your choice to wear it. And your journey to bear."

BACK OUTSIDE, the door chimed softly behind me, like a gentle farewell.

As I walked the cobbled streets of Coral Cove, the usual sounds faded beneath the pounding of my heart.

The ring sat in my pocket—silent, patient.

Yet somehow, it pulsed in rhythm with my steps.

A second heartbeat.

A promise.

Or maybe, a warning.

CHAPTER 2
HIM

S he is close."

The slipper hums in my hands, warm with recent magic, faintly glowing at its core. Starlight and bone—that's what it's made of. Not glass. Not really. The old stories always get it wrong. It's not about the foot. Not truly. It's about the bond.

The bloodline.

The pull.

The matching thread between curse and cure.

The last girl screamed.

I warned them not to force the fit. It's not meant to be jammed onto any girl with a pretty ankle and a noble name. It chooses. It *knows*. And when it does not find its match, it breaks them.

She cracked like porcelain.

I watched it happen.

And now the slipper is quiet again. Waiting.

The room I stand in is more crypt than court—its walls etched in ancient sigils, the floor a perfect ring of ironwood and salt. Shadows gather in the corners, thicker than they should be. Watching.

I place the slipper on the obsidian pedestal and close my eyes.

Show me.

The castle stirs around me.

There's no answer in words—only sensation. A chill across my collarbone. A flutter of warmth beneath my ribs. The glass hums louder, then quiets, then hums again.

She is not here.

Not yet.

But she is *close*.

I WALK the halls of Cairndale alone, my boots echoing against the stone. The portraits stare down at me—past brides, past offerings, past mistakes. Some smile. Most don't. One is blank, the canvas scraped clean.

I had it removed last winter. Couldn't bear the eyes anymore.

The castle's hunger grows with the turning

season. It needs a bride. A bond. A body tethered to the magic that keeps this place alive. I am the prince, yes—but only because I am its prisoner first. Its warden second.

The old blood built Cairndale as a fortress. Not just of stone, but of *intention*. Of bargain.

The cost of that bargain is steep.

And I am running out of time.

The coven sent another list. Names, ages, houses. Dozens of girls paraded like livestock. None of them will do. They never do.

I don't want another ceremony. Another fanfare. Another girl trying to impress me with soft eyes and obedient smiles.

I want truth.

Power.

Someone who does not flinch when they see what I am beneath the coat and crown.

And then—

I feel it.

A ripple in the air.

Magic.

Old. Unexpected. *Raw.*

It drags across my spine like a hook.

I turn toward the north tower, toward the heart of the castle where the artifact rests. The ring.

Someone just put it on.

Someone outside the boundary.

Someone *real*.

The mirror flares.

Her image appears—not fully formed, but enough. Auburn hair. Wide eyes. Fury in her mouth and longing in her bones.

I see her.

I *feel* her.

She is *perfect*.

The slipper pulses behind me.

It knows.

She is coming.

And Cairndale has just awakened.

CHAPTER 3
HER

Rage rolls through me like a storm as I step into my apartment, and my eyes land on the framed photos on the wall—the ones with Mark and his plastered-on grin beside me, trying his hardest to look like Prince Charming. They're the first to go. I rip them from the wall, tearing the photos right out of their frames, and shred each one to pieces until I'm left holding nothing but a pile of ripped paper and a fistful of fake memories.

What was I thinking all those months, pretending everything was fine? I could feel it, like an itch under my skin, that something was off with him. All his late "work nights," the secretive texts, and the way he'd pull his phone away like a teenage boy with a dirty magazine. And now, he has the nerve to look shocked when I catch him with Jenna?

Jenna.

I grit my teeth at the name, then turn my attention to the next pile of junk he left behind in my apartment.

In the hallway closet, I find his spare gym clothes, his half-empty bottle of cologne, and a stupid novelty mug he bought "just for me" that I never even liked. I throw it all in a trash bag with a finality that sends a thrill through me. If it wasn't for my mother's voice in my head, I'd light the whole pile on fire right here in my living room, watch it turn to ash and laugh as it smoldered. But as much as I hate to admit it, her words echo in my mind: *Polite ladies don't burn things, Ember.*

"Fuck polite," I mutter, a little too loudly, as I haul the bag of garbage outside to the dumpster. *I am so tired of being fucking polite.*

Standing there in the dim glow of the streetlight, I take a deep breath. This is supposed to be the part where I feel liberated, free from that idiot and the mind-numbing routine of pretending he was enough for me. But all I feel is anger and... emptiness. What a joke. For months, I was faking it. And I don't mean just pretending to be happy—I was faking *everything*. Mark was good at a lot of things, but making a woman feel wanted, truly desired? That was not one of them.

It's almost funny, in a pathetic sort of way. The only position he seemed to know was missionary, as if that was the grand finale of bedroom feats. And after about five minutes of puffing and grunting on top of me, he'd flop over with a self-satisfied grin, completely oblivious to the fact that I'd faked it just to get him to finish. I only climaxed twice the entire two years we were together, and even then, they were the saddest, weakest excuses for orgasms.

Good riddance to Mark and his boring, predictable, vanilla routine. I shake my head, finally feeling a small smile tug at the corners of my mouth. What I need is a real man, someone who isn't afraid of a woman who actually knows her own body and isn't shy about saying what she wants. Not some cowardly, self-centered man-child.

Back inside, I slump onto the couch, my anger mellowing into something almost bittersweet. I reach into my pocket, feeling the smooth, cool surface of the ring I bought earlier today from *Lilly Drake*. The weight of it seems to grow heavier in my hand, as if it's holding onto something, waiting for me. I glance down at the silver band, at the uncut stone that somehow seems to catch light even in the dimness of my apartment. It's mesmerizing, like a doorway to something else, something *better*. My fingers tingle, almost with a will of their own, as I slide the ring onto my finger.

The second it's on, a wave of warmth rushes up my arm, spreading through me in a way that makes the room spin. Colors blur, shapes twist and stretch, and for a moment, I think I'm going to pass out. But then, as suddenly as it began, the feeling fades, and I blink to find myself... somewhere else.

I'm no longer in my apartment. Instead, I'm standing on a cobbled street under a vast, star-speckled sky, the air alive with scents of lavender and freshly baked bread. The sky glows in shades of twilight, tinged with the faintest purple hues. Around me is a bustling town square, its edges lined with quaint little shops, their awnings colorful and inviting. The warm glow from their windows spills onto the street, casting an enchanting light over the scene, and every shop seems to have its own charm —a bakery with golden loaves stacked in the window, a flower stall bursting with colors, and a tiny apothecary with jars and vials that glitter in the lamplight.

Ahead of me, rising against the night like a towering dream, is a castle unlike anything I could have imagined. Its spires stretch skyward, draped in shadows that seem to deepen the further up they go, as if it's reaching into some hidden realm. A chill prickles down my spine as I take it in. Everything here feels otherworldly, like stepping into a fairytale —but there's an undercurrent to it all, something dark, humming beneath the surface.

I'm so taken in by the sight of the castle that I barely notice when a crowd sweeps past, guiding me into a line of women. Each one is dressed in finery, their expressions ranging from nervous to downright terrified. I look down at myself, realizing I'm wearing something unfamiliar—a gown of deep midnight blue, fitted to me like a second skin, the fabric soft and cool against my body. It's beautiful but unfamiliar, and for a second, I wonder if I'm dreaming. But the pressure of the ring on my finger reminds me that this is real.

"What's going on?" I ask the woman next to me, a petite girl with wide, frightened eyes.

She flinches, like the question itself is dangerous. Then she glances at me—really looks—and her expression shifts from fear to pity.

"It's the prince's decree," she whispers, voice barely audible over the hum of the crowd. "Every eligible woman must try on the slipper. If it fits..."

Her voice trails into a shiver, and she crosses

herself with trembling fingers, as if trying to ward off something ancient and cruel.

I raise an eyebrow. "What happens if it fits?"

Her gaze hardens, jaw tight. "You're taken to the castle. And no one ever sees you again."

I open my mouth to speak, but she cuts me off—urgently, like she's afraid she won't get another chance to warn me.

"They say the shoe is cursed," she whispers. "Old magic. Fae, probably. It's not just glass—it's starlight and bone, molded into a vessel for blood-binding. They say it *chooses* someone. Not for love, like in the stories, but for sacrifice. For power."

My skin prickles.

She keeps talking, her voice barely a breath. "Long ago, the royal bloodline made a pact. When their magic began to fade, they forged the slipper from the remains of the first girl it devoured. Every generation, the shoe awakens. It calls to one. The rest are spared. But the one it fits..." She swallows. "She goes to the prince. And then she vanishes."

I stare at her, heartbeat skittering.

"How do you know all this?" I ask.

She glances away, clutching the lace at her throat. "My sister was chosen last season."

My breath catches.

"What happened to her?"

Her lips tremble. "No one will say. Her name was scrubbed from the records. No burial. No letter. No body." She wipes at her eyes furiously. "It's like she never existed."

A ripple of unease trickles through me, winding tight around my ribs.

But instead of retreating, some part of me stirs— wild and reckless and starving for more.

Because even now, with every warning screaming run, I can't look away from that castle.

Can't silence the pull in my blood.

Maybe it's foolish. Maybe it's fatal.

But the life I had was already a slow death.

I straighten, gaze fixed on the looming silhouette in the distance. Whatever awaits me there—it will not be ordinary.

And I was never meant for ordinary.

The line shuffles forward, and I watch the women in front of me as they take their turn with the slipper, each one leaving with a visible sigh of relief when it doesn't fit. They whisper in hushed tones, glancing nervously at the attendants in dark clothing standing nearby. The whispers are barely audible, but I catch bits and pieces—something about the prince of *Cairndale*, a man said to be a monster clad in shadows. Rumor has it that no woman has left his castle alive, that he's dangerous, unpredictable, and as dark as the black he wears.

Finally, it's my turn. A tall, impossibly handsome man kneels before me, holding a single glass slipper in his hands. His features are sharp, chiseled, with an intensity that makes my heart skip a beat. His eyes are dark, unreadable, and as he looks up at me, something in his gaze makes the air between us crackle. He reaches for my ankle, his fingers brushing my skin, and the touch is electric, sending a thrill up my leg that I can't explain.

He slips the slipper onto my foot, and the fit is so perfect it's as if it were made for me. A hush falls over the crowd as he straightens, his gaze locked on mine, that devilishly handsome smile curving his lips. He doesn't speak, but there's a promise in his eyes—a dangerous, intoxicating promise that makes my pulse race.

"What does this mean?" I ask, my voice barely more than a whisper, though I can't mask the curiosity laced through it. "And who exactly is everyone talking about?"

His smile widens, a touch of something wicked glinting in his eyes. "It means, my lady, that you are chosen. And it means you are about to meet the prince."

The words settle over me, heavy and thrilling. As

his hand lingers on my calf, slowly trailing upward, I feel a pull between us, a tension I've never felt with anyone before. Whatever this prince may be— monster or man—I can't deny the allure.

Mark's fumbling hands, his predictable routine, feel like a distant memory. This world, this adventure—it's exactly what I was looking for. The man before me gives my calf a gentle squeeze, his touch lingering before he lets go, and I know, without a doubt, that whatever lies ahead will be anything but ordinary.

CHAPTER 4

HIM

"It fits."

I feel it before I see it. The castle trembles—subtle, like a held breath.

Then the slipper shudders in my hand. Warm. Alive.

The fit is perfect.

Not just physically. *Magically.*

The spell latches with a snap like a wolf's jaw closing on prey.

I lift my gaze to the woman before me, the slipper still cradled in my palm, the soft curve of her ankle still under my hand.

She doesn't flinch. Not when our skin touches. Not when the air around us thickens like a closing throat.

She's... stunning. But that's not what matters.

She feels *real*.

She feels *true*.

And gods, she is angry.

I see it in her eyes, even through the haze of confusion. There's a storm in her, one that hasn't broken yet. One I want to stand in the center of.

I rise slowly, letting her see the truth in my face —the recognition. The certainty.

The slipper still hums, bound now to her. It will not fit another.

She is mine.

The procession begins at once.

My men know their roles. The town knows its cues. It is theater—elegant, polished, and under-pinned by centuries of fear.

The trumpet blares.

She stands alone.

The crowd cheers, but it is not joy. It is a ritual of survival.

They clap because if they don't, the castle *listens*.

I watch from the shadows as she's flanked by two guards. She doesn't try to flee. She walks with them—warily, but willingly. Her posture is rigid with tension. Her lips are set.

Already, she is stronger than most.

The others cried.

Some fainted.

She keeps her head high.

The crowd begins to murmur. Whispers coil around her like fog.

"She doesn't know what he is."

"Poor girl. Look at her, all fire. The castle will eat that first."

I do not blame them.

They've seen too many disappear.

They don't understand that *this one is different*.

Not yet.

The carriage waiting for her is obsidian-polished and rune-bound. Its horses are trained not with bridles, but with bloodline and whisper. When she climbs inside, the spell locks behind her with a flicker of silver across the door.

I walk the walls above as she rides toward the castle.

The forest leans in as she passes. It recognizes her. *Marks* her.

Somewhere in its branches, the wildfolk stir. Old things blink open their eyes and whisper her name to the dirt.

Ember.

She does not know what that name means here.

But she will.

I AM WAITING on the steps when the carriage arrives.

The castle shifts under my feet.

The door opens.

She steps out, gown rustling, firelight catching in her hair.

And gods, she is even more than I imagined.

She looks up at the castle like it's a challenge.

Like it will blink first.

I nearly smile.

Good.

I do not want a lamb.

I want the *girl who will burn me alive*.

She does not see me.

Not yet.

She's ushered inside by the stewards, and I stay in the shadows, watching her footsteps echo through my hall. Watching the moment she passes beneath the arch of the throne wing.

The castle marks her passage. Its wards flicker. The ancient magic *tastes* her.

It knows.

She will not break like the others.

She will not kneel easily.

And I—

I want to see how far she will go before she refuses me outright.

Because that moment—when she bares her teeth, when she says no, when she throws the first blow?

That will be the moment I truly fall.

CHAPTER 5
HER

The trumpet blares—shrill and sudden—like a slap to the face.

It yanks me out of the haze and drops me hard into the now.

I'm standing at the center of the square, surrounded by the same women I'd waited with moments ago. But now?

They're stepping back.

Not like I'm royalty.

Like I'm a warning.

Then the cheering starts.

Too loud. Too sudden. It crashes over me like waves that don't match the tide. The sound is all wrong—hollow and rehearsed.

People line the cobbled streets, their eyes fixed on me.

Some look curious.

Some, wary.

Others—especially the women—look away entirely. Their lips press into hard, grim lines.

Not one of them smiles.

Two men in black appear beside me. Their expressions are carved from stone, their suits too stiff, too still. They flank me like guards, like shadows, like fate made flesh.

And I walk.

I don't know why I follow. Maybe because I don't know where else to go.

Maybe because part of me still wants to know where this path leads.

The air is thick with an unfamiliar scent—floral but sharp, like crushed petals with a bite of iron. It sinks into my lungs. Into my skin.

I feel it lodge in my bones like a spell.

A parade. For me.

Part of me wants to laugh.

To twirl like a fairytale princess and wink at the crowd.

But I don't.

Because something about the way they look at me makes my stomach twist.

Their clapping is mechanical. Compulsory.

I see it in their eyes.

Not celebration.

Mourning.

They whisper behind their hands, not bothering to hide it.

"Poor thing," murmurs a woman as she pulls her child closer.

"Another one for the prince," a man mutters, shaking his head. "She won't last a week."

"She's a goner," someone else says softly. "Didn't even get a choice."

My breath catches in my throat.

I glance over my shoulder, half-hoping—half-foolishly hoping—I'll see a way out.

There's none.

The crowd is too thick. The guards too close.

The slipper too perfect.

The street blurs as I walk. We pass vendors selling sugared pears and charm-stitched bracelets, but no one hawks their wares. No one calls out.

Their hands clap harder.

Their faces stay blank.

I'm nudged forward, one gloved hand resting against my back. Gentle, but firm. Firm enough to say: you go forward, and nowhere else.

My heart pounds. Each beat a countdown.

Ahead, a carriage waits—black wood polished to a gleam, silver accents that catch the light like broken glass. The horses are massive, their coats midnight-dark, their eyes... wrong. Too aware. Too human.

One of the men takes my arm.

He helps me into the carriage like I'm made of porcelain. Like they're doing me a kindness.

The door shuts behind me with a soft, final click.

Inside, the air is warm and heavy, laced with rose petals and something metallic—something sharp.

The cushions are velvet, lush and dark as ink.

The kind of luxury that feels more like a trap than a gift.

I press my fingers to the window, watching as the crowd fades.

Even through the glass, I can hear the whispers.

The prince eats their hearts.

He drains them.

He breaks them until they forget their names.

The carriage lurches forward.

I lean back, gripping the edge of the seat as the streets give way to forest.

The trees grow denser.

Branches twist above us, gnarled into a canopy that swallows the sun.

Shadows pool like blood on the path.

I try to summon memories of Coral Cove. The

scent of saltwater. The sound of seagulls. My tiny apartment, cluttered but safe.

But it all slips through my fingers like sand.

Like it never really existed.

Like I never really existed.

The castle looms ahead.

And gods, it's worse up close.

Its walls are obsidian—not painted dark, but born dark, forged from something ancient and unsympathetic. The stone drinks the light.

Its towers pierce the sky like the ribs of some ancient beast.

The carriage halts.

Before I can move, the door opens, and the guards are there again—guiding me, silent as shadows.

The castle doors open not with sound, but with pressure. A pull, as if the building breathes.

I step inside.

The floor is polished marble, black-veined and cold. Torches line the hall, but their flames flicker low, casting shadows that stretch and twitch like they have minds of their own.

Everything is too still.

Too clean.

Like the place is waiting. Watching. Hungry.

A woman appears from the dark. She glides

toward me in a gown black as pitch, her long hair pinned into a crown of braids. She's older—but not fragile. Regal. Composed.

Her expression is unreadable.

"Welcome," she says.

Her voice echoes through the vast hall like a chime in a crypt.

"You are here as the prince's guest. I will show you to your chambers."

Guest.

The word hangs there like smoke. Brittle. False.

Still, I nod.

I follow her down a long corridor lined with faded tapestries—battlefields soaked in red thread, queens with eyes like knives, kings with swords raised in triumph and blood.

We stop at a door.

She opens it with one hand.

"Your quarters. You will remain here until summoned. Meals will be brought. If you need anything, ring the bell."

I nod again, but she's already gone. The door closes with a quiet click—not loud. Just certain.

I stand there, alone.

Waiting.

The room is beautiful. Richly appointed.

But every luxury feels like a velvet cage.

The bed is massive, canopied in midnight silks. A fire crackles in the hearth, casting dancing light across the high walls.

A mirror stands tall and gleaming, its frame carved with wolves and roses and thorns.

I don't trust it.

I move to the window and part the curtains.

Below, the town is a distant flicker of light.

It looks so small. So fragile.

Like something I dreamed and forgot.

I press my fingers to the cold glass.

What have I done?

I sit by the fire.

The room is too quiet. The flames are the only sound—crackling, whispering like they know secrets I don't.

I think about the townspeople's faces.

The way they looked at me like I was already dead.

They weren't cheering.

They were grieving.

They weren't celebrating.

They were surrendering.

And now I'm here.

In a castle of shadows.

Wearing the ring I chose to put on.

Foolish? Maybe.

Reckless? Absolutely.

But I'm not sorry.

Because whatever's coming, at least I won't die bored in Coral Cove, faking orgasms and pretending I don't want more.

I touch the ring again.

Its surface is smooth. Cold.

It pulses faintly under my thumb.

This isn't a fairytale.

This is something darker. Wilder. Hungrier.

Let the prince come.

Let him try to intimidate me.

I didn't come here to be saved.

I came here to burn.

CHAPTER 6
HER

T he bathwater is warm, nearly hot, and scented with something floral and sweet, like jasmine and roses, but with a hint of something spicier underneath. I sink into it, feeling the tension melt from my muscles as I recline in the massive, stone-carved tub. Around me, steam rises in delicate tendrils, wrapping me in its embrace as the soft hum of water fills the air.

Two attendants—silent, watchful women with calm, unreadable expressions—work carefully, their hands gentle as they pour fragrant oils into the water and lather my skin with soaps that smell almost too divine to be real. Their movements are methodical, practiced, and strangely soothing, each stroke a reminder of how far I am from the ordinary.

One woman rinses my hair, her fingers

massaging my scalp with a tenderness that makes my eyes drift closed. Another works a cloth along my arms and shoulders, the warm water and soft touch making my skin come alive, heightening every sensation. This world is so new, so lush, and as strange as it is, I let myself sink into the experience, letting the last remnants of Coral Cove dissolve away.

When I open my eyes, I meet the gaze of one of the attendants, her expression solemn but with the barest hint of warmth. "The prince wishes you to look your finest," she says, her voice soft, yet each word carries a weight that lingers. "Tonight is your introduction."

Her words send a jolt of nervousness through me, but also a spark of anticipation that flutters low in my belly. I nod, letting them continue as they comb oils through my hair, leaving it sleek and shining, before wrapping me in a soft robe and leading me to a large dressing room. There, an intricate gown awaits—its fabric deep shades of midnight blue that shimmer when the light hits just right, as if woven with threads of moonlight. The bodice is tight and fitted, its neckline dipping just enough to be alluring without crossing into scandalous, and the skirts flow with an elegance that feels timeless.

They lace me into it, the fabric molding to my

body as though it were made just for me. The weight of the gown, its texture, the feel of it against my skin —it's intoxicating, and as I look at myself in the mirror, I hardly recognize the woman staring back. I look like someone from a dream, someone I've always wanted to be.

My heart races as they place a delicate silver chain around my neck, its charm a small, dark gem that mirrors the ring on my finger. I touch it, feeling the cool metal, letting it ground me. The attendants step back, admiring their work before nodding to each other in approval.

"You are ready," one of them says, and the words feel like a summons, an invitation to something far beyond my understanding.

They escort me through a series of dimly lit corridors, their silence only heightening my sense of expectation. The air grows cooler as we move deeper into the castle, and I can hear the faint hum of voices ahead, low and murmuring. We arrive at a set of large, ornately carved doors, and the attendants stop, giving me a look that feels almost like a warning before one of them knocks, the sound echoing through the hall.

The doors open, and I step into a grand hall filled with people, their eyes all turning toward me as I enter. I feel their stares, some curious, others critical, but I force myself to stand tall, to let the weight of the gown and the confidence it lends carry me forward.

At the far end of the hall, standing alone, is the man who fit the slipper to my foot. His eyes are dark, intense, and they find mine with a precision that makes me shiver. He's dressed in black, a long, fitted coat that accentuates his tall, lean form, with silver detailing along the collar and cuffs that glints under the chandeliers' light. His hair is as dark as night, falling slightly over his brow, framing a face that's all sharp angles and piercing eyes that seem to look right through me.

A thrill runs through me, undeniable and unbidden. The memory of his touch, that electric brush of his fingers against my skin, floods back, and my cheeks warm as I recall the look in his eyes then— knowing, confident, as if he had already claimed me.

He watches me with a half-smile, his gaze unwavering, drawing me toward him with an intensity that makes my heart race. The crowd fades away, and all I can see is him, the dark prince of Cairndale, the man with the reputation that's haunted my thoughts since I arrived. The whispers I heard in the town—of cruelty, of magic and power —surround me, lingering in my mind as I step forward.

"Welcome, Ember," he says, his voice a low rumble that feels like it travels through me, sinking into my bones. He steps forward, reaching for my hand, his grip firm yet gentle as he brings it to his lips, his gaze never leaving mine. His eyes are impossibly dark, but within them, I see glints of something unreadable, something dangerous. I can't tear my eyes away.

"Your Highness," I manage, my voice softer than I intended, but steady. His lips curve into a smile, one that feels like it's meant just for me.

"You're even lovelier than I anticipated," he says, his tone smooth, almost soothing, but there's a flicker of something sharper beneath his words, a hint of darkness that sends a shiver through me. "And courageous, to have come so willingly."

I swallow, feeling the weight of his hand on mine, the warmth of his skin. "I wasn't aware I had a choice," I reply, a touch of defiance in my tone.

His smile widens, a glint of amusement in his eyes. "Ah, but choices are often not as clear as we'd like them to be. You're here now, and that, dear Ember, speaks volumes."

The room falls silent as he leads me to the center of the hall, where a dais awaits, draped in dark velvet. He stands beside me, his presence overwhelming, and I feel the weight of every gaze in the room upon us, every whisper held back as they wait for his next move.

"Tonight, we celebrate the arrival of our future princess," he announces, his voice carrying through the hall, commanding every ear, every eye. A murmur ripples through the crowd, and I catch glimpses of their expressions—some curious, others fearful, a few downright hostile. The knowledge that I am their future princess hangs heavy over me, both thrilling and terrifying.

He turns to me, his gaze steady, his hand still holding mine. "You are here because you were chosen," he says, his voice lower, meant only for me. "But the path forward will not be easy. This is a kingdom of shadows and secrets, a place where loyalty and courage are paramount." He tilts his head, studying me, his dark eyes searching mine. "Are you prepared for that, Ember?"

His question lingers in the air between us, and I feel the weight of it, the pull of something deep and magnetic drawing me closer. I barely know this man, but I can't deny the force of his presence, the way his touch makes my heart race, the way his voice seems to sink into my skin.

"Yes," I say, the word escaping before I even realize it. "I am."

His lips curve into that same half-smile, pleased

yet mysterious. "Good. Because this journey will test you, in ways you cannot yet imagine." He steps closer, his gaze intensifying, and I feel the warmth of his breath as he leans in, his voice a low whisper against my ear. "But know this, in Cairndale, loyalty is rewarded. And disobedience... punished."

The words send a shiver down my spine, a thrill and a warning all wrapped into one. His hand lingers on mine, his fingers tracing the line of my wrist, and I feel my pulse quicken under his touch. His scent reaches me—a dark, intoxicating blend of something woodsy, maybe cedar, with a hint of smoke and spice. It's a scent that makes me want to lean closer, to breathe him in.

"You are mine now, Ember," he says softly, his words possessive yet gentle, as if claiming me with both strength and tenderness. "Tonight is only the beginning."

I look up at him, my heart pounding, caught between the thrill of his touch and the lingering whispers of his reputation. Part of me wants to pull away, to run, to reclaim some semblance of control. But another part—the part that's been drawn to him from the moment he slipped that glass slipper onto my foot—wants nothing more than to stay, to follow him into whatever shadows he's promising.

The crowd claps as he raises our joined hands,

and the sound swells around us, a hollow echo in the grand hall. He doesn't release me, guiding me down from the dais and back through the crowd, our exit watched by hundreds of eyes, yet all I can feel is him, his touch, his warmth.

When we reach the edge of the hall, he pauses, his eyes locking onto mine once more. "Rest tonight, Ember. Tomorrow, you'll begin to understand what it truly means to be part of Cairndale." His tone is final, a promise that verges on threat, and as much as it chills me, it excites me even more.

He releases my hand, and the attendants reappear, bowing as they gesture for me to follow them. I take one last look at him, the dark prince of Cairndale, standing amidst the shadows, his gaze fixed on me with a possession that feels almost feral.

CHAPTER 7
HIM

*S*he is in the castle now.

And the walls can't stop whispering her name.

The torches burn lower. The air grows heavier. The castle hums with recognition. Not fear—anticipation.

Cairndale remembers her.

Even if she doesn't remember *it*.

I sit in the west tower, boots propped on the arm of a centuries-old chair, sipping wine as dark as blood. The mirror beside me shows flashes of her—drifting between corridors, wrapped in velvet and silence, the attendants washing the world from her skin.

She has not cried.

She has not begged.

She closes her eyes during the bath, not from fear... but pleasure.

Bold thing.

The last girl screamed when they drew her a bath—convinced it was poison.

But this one? She melts into it like she belongs.

Maybe she does.

I RISE as the sky darkens. Dusk bleeds violet through the high windows.

The black coat is laid out for me—tailored to my shoulders, embroidered at the cuffs with silver thread woven from moonlight and ash. I run my hand along the lapel, where the sigil of Cairndale is stitched: a thorned crown over a broken star.

Tonight, they expect a performance.

They will get something far more dangerous.

I descend the marble stairs in silence, the heels of my boots striking rhythm into the stone.

The guards bow. The hall quiets.

She is behind the great doors, just on the other side.

I can feel her heartbeat.

Not metaphorically—literally. The castle's bond

allows it now. The slipper changed everything. Her pulse is quick—elevated. Not panicked.

Excited.

Good.

Let her come to me on shaking legs, but with her spine unbent.

I take my place at the far end of the great hall, alone beneath the chandeliers, where shadows cling to the velvet drapery and the silence stretches long.

And then—

the doors open.

SHE STEPS IN.

And everything stops.

Conversation halts. Movement ceases. Even the fire seems to burn quieter in her presence.

She is... breathtaking.

Midnight blue silk clings to her like it was sewn by starlight. Her skin glows against it. Her eyes—those stormlit eyes—scan the crowd without flinching.

A queen in a room full of jackals.

When her gaze finds mine, the connection snaps into place. That invisible tether tightens, pulling her forward like gravity has shifted to obey *me*.

Every step she takes toward me feels like a test

she's passing with ease. She is elegance sharpened into defiance.

And gods help me, I want her even more now than I did before.

Not just her beauty—though it could stop armies.

I want her anger.

Her fire.

Her refusal.

"Welcome, Ember," I say, my voice low enough to make her lean in, sharp enough to silence the room.

She answers me softly, but not weakly. "Your Highness."

I take her hand.

And I do not kiss it.

I *claim* it.

My lips brush skin, and magic flares across our bond like a match striking dry parchment.

"You're even lovelier than I anticipated," I murmur.

She doesn't smile.

"I wasn't aware I had a choice," she replies. There's steel in her voice, polished and precise.

I almost laugh.

Almost.

"Choice," I say, "is an illusion. But you're here now. And that speaks volumes."

I lead her up to the dais.

Every gaze in the room is on us—some hopeful, some hostile, all afraid.

They know what this means.

The bond has been made. The castle has accepted her.

And if she survives...

She'll be the most powerful consort this realm has seen in a generation.

"Tonight," I announce, my voice a dark bell tolling through the vaulted ceiling, "we welcome the future princess of Cairndale."

I hear the sharp intake of breath from nobles who'd planned for their daughters to wear this crown. I feel their fear. Good.

She will need that fear.

I lean in. My lips nearly graze her ear.

"This kingdom thrives on secrets," I whisper. "On power. Loyalty will keep you safe. Rebellion will not."

She meets my gaze.

She does not look away.

"Are you prepared for that, Ember?" I ask.

Her answer is soft.

But it is sure.

"Yes," she says.

Mine, the castle whispers. *Ours.*

I smile slowly, hunger coiling in my gut like smoke.

"Good. Because you are mine now. And tonight is only the beginning."

CHAPTER 8
HER

The attendants escorted me back to my chambers after the ceremony and closed the door behind me with a soft but definitive click. A lock sliding into place. Not loud. Not threatening. Just... final.

I test it anyway.

The door doesn't budge.

Neither do the windows.

I'm caged in silk and shadow.

I stand at the window, staring out over the dark landscape of Cairndale. It's breathtaking—moon-silver light gleaming across spires and towers, the woods beyond stretching like ink across parchment. But the longer I look, the more I feel the weight of it. The beauty here is a mask. It conceals something vast. Something watching.

The room is exquisite. Velvet, gold leaf, flickering firelight. Everything hand-selected for comfort, for seduction.

And yet... every hair on my body stands on end.

I've been locked inside a gilded cage.

And the hunter already knows I'm here.

I turn away from the window and pace the room, my bare feet silent against the polished floor. I can still feel his hand on mine from the ceremony. The press of his lips. The words he spoke—his promise of reward for loyalty and punishment for defiance.

They weren't empty threats.

I felt it.

Something in him hums with power barely contained. Something not entirely human.

A knock at the door makes me jump.

When it opens, a young woman slips inside. Pale and small, her movements quick but precise—like someone used to being punished for taking up space.

"My lady," she says with a bow, barely raising her eyes. "I'm Liana. I'm here to tend to you... if you need anything."

There's a strain behind her composure. Her voice is steady, but something in her posture—shoulders tight, chin low—gives her away.

She places a tray on the table. Tea. Pastries. A delicate silver spoon beside a porcelain cup. Everything designed to soothe.

But nothing about this place is safe.

"Thank you, Liana," I say softly, sitting down. "Will you stay and talk with me?"

She hesitates.

Then nods.

She remains standing, hands folded, but her body stays angled toward the door like she might bolt at any second.

I lower my voice. "Liana... I heard the whispers. About the prince. About the other women."

Her eyes widen. Her breath catches.

For a moment, I think she'll deny everything.

Instead, she checks the door, then steps closer.

"They say no one ever leaves," she whispers, eyes darting like moths. "That he draws them in with magic. With the slipper. And once they're bound—he uses them. For power. For something darker."

The room suddenly feels colder.

"Uses them how?" I ask.

She bites her lip, looks away.

"Some say... he feeds on them. Their magic. Their energy. Their hearts."

I clutch the teacup tighter.

"What is he?"

Liana swallows. "Cursed. That's the rumor. Not fully man. Not anymore."

I want to tell her it's ridiculous.

But I can't.

Because I saw something in his eyes.

Something ancient. And hungry.

"Has he hurt anyone?" I ask, almost dreading the answer.

"I don't know." Her voice is barely a breath. "But the others... the ones who came before... they're gone."

A pause.

Then her hand brushes mine—soft and brief.

"Be careful," she whispers. "Promise me."

"I promise," I say. But the lie tastes bitter.

Because I won't be careful.

I'm already too deep.

When Liana leaves, I'm alone again.

The fire crackles softly, shadows dancing across the ceiling. I sit in the velvet chair and sip the tea, trying to anchor myself. But my thoughts keep returning to him.

To the way he looked at me like I was already his.

To the part of me that wanted to be.

Sleep won't come.

My body is restless, strung tight like a bow.

Then—

A sound.

Soft. Subtle. Like breath on stone.

I sit up. My heart stutters.

He's there.

The prince.

Standing in the shadows by the door, his presence thick and charged. His expression unreadable. His body relaxed—but his gaze is anything but.

Predatory.

Dangerous.

Irresistible.

"Couldn't sleep?" he asks, voice like smoke.

"No," I whisper. "I've been thinking."

"About me?" A slow, wicked smile. The room seems to shrink with every step he takes toward me.

I should run.

I don't.

"Yes," I say.

He sits at the edge of the bed. Close enough that I can feel the heat of him. His fingers lift—tracing the line of my collarbone, feather-light but electric.

"You're curious," he murmurs, "about what I am... and what I'll do to you."

His hand moves to my shoulder, brushing the fabric aside, grazing bare skin. I shiver beneath his touch.

"I've heard the stories," I breathe.

"And yet..." he leans closer, his lips just above mine, "here you are."

His fingers trail along my jaw.

"I don't know what to believe."

"Then believe what you feel."

His hand slides into my hair, firm and commanding. My breath catches. He tilts my face toward his, and I see something in his eyes—desire, yes, but something deeper.

Possession.

Recognition.

"Tell me you want this," he whispers, his voice a low, intoxicating murmur. "Tell me you feel it too."

I part my lips, my breath catching as his hand trails down to my neck, his fingers tracing the delicate line of my collarbone. Every nerve in my body is on edge, every thought drowned out by the sensation of his touch, the overwhelming pull of him. "I... I do," I admit, my voice trembling, but the words are true. I can't deny it. I'm drawn to him, as dangerous as he may be, as much as the whispers haunt me.

His smile deepens, a flash of something dark and satisfied crossing his face as he leans in, his lips brushing against the curve of my neck, his breath warm against my skin. "Good," he murmurs, his voice like a dark promise, his hand moving to my waist, his grip firm, possessive. "Because once you're mine... there's no turning back."

I close my eyes, my body melting into his touch, the warmth of his hand on my waist grounding me even as my mind races. The fear lingers, but it's muted, overwhelmed by the rush of desire that floods through me, the inexplicable need to be closer to him, to know every hidden part of him.

His hand moves to my jaw, tilting my face up to meet his gaze, and for a moment, he just looks at me, his dark eyes filled with an intensity that makes my heart skip a beat. "You belong here, Ember," he whispers, his lips brushing against mine, his voice filled with a strange tenderness that contrasts with the darkness in his gaze. "You belong with me."

And then he kisses me. His lips are warm, soft yet demanding, and I feel myself melt into him, surrendering to the pull between us, to the promises and the dangers that lie within his touch. His hand slides down to my back, pulling me closer, and I feel the strength in his grip, the possessiveness, the certainty that he knows exactly what he's doing to me.

Every touch, every whispered word blurs the line

between fear and desire, between caution and surrender, and I find myself lost in him, in the darkness and the thrill that he embodies. Whatever he is, whatever secrets he holds, I want to know them, to uncover every part of him, even if it means losing myself in the process.

As his hands trace paths along my skin, his touch both gentle and possessive, I realize that there's no going back. I'm his, bound to him by a connection I don't fully understand, drawn to him despite the warnings and the fear. And as the night stretches on, I know one thing for certain: he's claimed me, and I don't want him to let go.

CHAPTER 9
HIM

She said yes.

Not with the careful submission the others wore like armor.

Not with fear in her voice.

She said it with trembling lips and burning eyes.

And she meant it.

That's what undoes me.

Not the softness.

Not the heat.

But the *truth* in her voice when she said, "I do."

I should have left.

I should have slipped into her chamber, spoken my piece, and disappeared into shadow. But the moment I saw her curled on that velvet chair, eyes glittering like stormlight, tea cradled between her hands—I knew I wouldn't leave.

She looked at me like I was already in her dreams.

I stepped from the shadows and she didn't scream.

She *invited me closer*.

The others always screamed.

She asked about the whispers.

The vanished brides.

The curse.

I could've lied. I've done it before.

But there was no need.

She already knows.

Even if her mind hasn't caught up with her blood, her soul has recognized me. I saw it when she sat up in bed. When I touched her throat. When she whispered that trembling, devastating truth:

"I do."

I could feel her pulse beneath my fingers.

Quick. Unsteady. Wanting.

I should be gentle with her.

But I'm not built for gentleness.

Not anymore.

My hand skimmed her waist and she didn't pull away. My mouth grazed her neck and she leaned in. When I asked her if she felt it too, she looked at me like I was a riddle she wanted to solve *with her body*.

She is not a lamb.

She is not prey.

She is a match waiting to be struck.

And I intend to burn with her.

When I kissed her, the castle reacted.

It always does when a choice is made.

But this time—there was no resistance.

The wards did not hiss.

The walls did not moan.

The stone *purred*.

She belongs here.

As my hands moved over her, I felt the shift begin. Not in her. *In me.*

Her mouth parted beneath mine and I tasted fire. She melted into me like we'd done this a hundred times before. Like her body remembered things her mind had never been taught.

I felt the bond pulse beneath my ribs—an ancient, hungry thread stretching taut between us.

But there's danger in it.

Not just for her.

For me.

Because the castle might want her for power.

But I want her for *more*.

She is not just a vessel.

Not just a bride.

She is the first thing I've *wanted* in years. Not to devour. Not to control.

To know.

To keep.

To *deserve*.

And that's what terrifies me most.

When I pull back to look at her, her lips are bruised and perfect. Her pupils blown wide. Her skin flushed like flame beneath snow.

She's mine.

But the question still remains...

Will I be hers?

CHAPTER 10

HER

The morning of my wedding dawns with a sky painted in silver and violet. Heavy clouds roll over the horizon like slow-moving waves, threatening to devour the light.

I sit before the grand mirror, silent as Liana pins a dark rose in my hair—its bloom near-black, a bruise of shadow nestled in my curls. I barely recognize the reflection staring back. The gown is gold and silver, woven with moonlight and illusion. Every stitch whispers power, beauty, sacrifice.

"Breathtaking, my lady," Liana murmurs.

I nod, my fingers clutching the edge of the dressing table. "Thank you," I say softly. "I... think I'll need it."

· · ·

THE GRAND HALL has been transformed.

Dark roses spill from silver vases, their petals deep as dried blood. Candlelight flickers from towering sconces, casting shadows like reaching fingers along the stone walls. The air hums with reverence—and dread.

The guests fall silent as I enter.

At the far end of the aisle stands the prince. His coat is black, tailored to perfection, silver embroidery winding across the collar like frost. His eyes meet mine, and something feral stirs inside me.

A thrill. A warning.

I walk forward, each step a surrender, each breath a vow.

The officiant is ancient. His robes shimmer like starlight caught in ink. His voice, low and resonant, echoes through the space like prophecy.

"This is a bond not merely of love," he says, "but of loyalty, of power, and of purpose. In the presence of shadow and flame, you will swear to each other vows that cannot be broken."

The prince lifts my hand.

"Ember," he says, his voice velvet-wrapped steel, "I vow to give you everything your heart dares to desire—power, protection, passion. I will be your strength when you falter. Your fire when the world runs cold. And in return..." He kisses my fingers. "I ask for your loyalty. Your courage. Your heart. Once you are mine, there is no release. We are bound— eternally."

The weight of his words falls over me like a spell.

I whisper my vow in return: "I vow to stand beside you in light and in darkness. To be your equal, your shadow, your flame. I give you my loyalty, my trust... and my heart."

The officiant seals it with a chant I do not understand.

But my soul does.

Magic pulses through the room. The bond is forged.

HE TAKES my hand and leads me through a long corridor. No words. Just his grip, steady and unyielding.

We reach a set of dark double doors. He throws them open.

Candlelight spills across a room dressed in shadow and silk. Roses are scattered across the floor. The air is thick with something heady—like wine and smoke and want.

He closes the door behind us.

The air grows thick as he steps toward me, his gaze burning with an intensity that leaves me breathless, every inch of his focus heavy, deliberate. My heart pounds, anticipation simmering beneath my skin, as he reaches out and his hands find my shoulders, large and warm, holding me in a way that is both grounding and electrifying. His touch trails down the delicate fabric of my gown, and with a single powerful motion, he grips the gold silk and tears it open, the sound of ripping fabric filling the air, raw and thrilling.

The torn gown slips away, baring me completely, and a shiver races through me as his eyes sweep over me, dark and hungry, claiming. The way he looks at me, like I am something precious yet possessed, ignites a thrill that winds through my entire being, leaving me breathless, wanting.

He steps closer, and his hands trail over my bare skin, his touch unyielding, authoritative, setting my senses alight. I feel myself leaning into him, surrendering to the magnetic pull between us, as any lingering fear dissolves, replaced by a need that burns just as fiercely as his. The strength in his grip, the intensity in his gaze—it's everything I never knew I wanted, a wild passion that consumes, and I find myself yearning for more, ready to be his in every way.

His fingers trace along my jaw, tilting my face up to meet his gaze, his lips curving into a dark, possessive smile. "You're mine, Ember," he murmurs, his voice a low, dangerous whisper. "Tonight... and every night to come."

HE LEANS DOWN, his lips brushing over mine, his touch demanding and somehow tender, as if he's both claiming me and giving himself over to me. His hands roam over my body, exploring, marking, leaving trails of heat that ignite something fierce and wild within me.

His mouth found mine and I was lost to his kiss. His tongue parted my lips finding my own sending a rush of warmth through every inch of my body. His strength, is raw power flowing through him, and I crave it. I need it. He pulls me closer, his body pressed against mine, every inch of him firm and unyielding.

Our breaths mingle, the room filled with the soft sounds of our movements, the low hum of our shared desire. I rip his shirt off him, and a sparkle in his eyes tells me I've done good. I surrender to him, to the darkness and the passion he offers, letting myself be swept away in the current of his touch, the thrill of his kiss. There's a possessiveness in his movements, a fierceness that borders on cruelty, yet beneath it, I sense a strange, twisted tenderness, a promise that he will be both my protector and my captor.

"Lay back," he demands guiding my body to the position he craves. My torso laid on the bed, as he spreads my legs apart. "Your pussy glistens with arousal.

I cleared my throat looking for words but none come.

I nod, watching him.

My cheeks flush as his hands find hips and he leans down to smell me.

"You're ripe fruit," his words are almost a growl. He licks my center and a moan escapes me. "You like that, don't you. I'm going to eat your cunt and then I'm going to fuck you until you come. Then I'm going to fuck you again." He smacks my ass and the sting of it sends vibrations through my clit.

"Yes please, sir," I manage.

"What a good girl you are," he says before his tongue finds my center and I'm lost to the magic of his touch. Ecstasy raddle brain, my breathing comes in short clipped breaths and I dig my fingers into the bed. The coiling in my center is violent, nearly forcing my brain and body to part ways with the sheer pleasure of it.

His mouth returns to mine, a fierce, consuming

kiss that seals his intent. I can taste myself on his tongue and lips—honey and pomegranate.

When he breaks the kiss he unbuckles his pants, letting them plop to the ground in a pile, revealing his full girth to me.

For the first time fear grips my body. He's not only long, but thick. I'm not sure his cock will fit. And if it does, will it rip through me? Is this why the women never return to town—his raging roided cock?

He guides me, his hands strong on my hips, flipping me over, now face down on the bed my ass in the air. The room is charged with our passion, each breath heavier than the last. I feel the bed's edge against my thighs, the coolness of the sheets in stark contrast to the heat of our bodies.

I can't think past the thickness of his monstrous erect cock.

He positions himself behind me, his hands gripping my hips tightly. I can feel the hardness of him pressing urgently between my legs, teasing at the entrance that aches for him. He leans over me, his breath hot against the nape of my neck, whispering fiercely, "Ready?"

Without waiting for my answer, he enters me, a single powerful thrust that makes me gasp and clutch at the sheets. He gives me only a moment to adjust before pulling out and thrusting inside me again.

His movements are relentless, deep, each stroke pushing me further into a delirium of pleasure. The bed creaks under our combined weight, his pace unyielding, every thrust punctuated by my soft cries.

"You're mine," he growls, each word punctuated with a deep, deliberate thrust of his cock. "Say it."

I can barely form words, lost in the sensations. He doesn't let up and the coiling in my entire body grows tighter.

"Say it," he demands, his words were laced with a darkness I needed more of.

I manage a breathy, "Yours," that seemed to drive him even further. His hand slips around, finding the bundle of nerves at my center. He begins a rhythm there that matches his thrusts, and the room blurs into a cacophony of sounds—the slap of skin, our uneven breaths, the faint noise of the storm outside echoing my own storm within.

The pressure builds, unbearable in its intensity, until it feels like I might shatter under the force of my own climax. "Please," I gasp, the word a keening plea that's half-lost in the depth of my throat.

"That's it," he murmurs, his voice rough with his own restraint. "Beg me to stop."

But I can't, I won't—each word dissolves into a moan as he brings me to the edge and then over it. My world explodes into brilliant shards of pleasure, each wave cresting higher than the last, until I'm crying out, not for him to stop, but for more, always more.

He follows soon after, a low, guttural sound marking his release as he fills me with his seed. When he's finished he collapses over me, our sweat-mingled bodies a testament to the rawness of our encounter. We stay like that, a tangle of limbs and heavy breaths, as the echoes of our passion fade into the stormy night outside.

Later, lying in his arms, the sheets twisted around us, the promise fulfilled, he kisses my shoulder and murmurs, "Was that what you wanted?"

All I can do is nod. As the night stretches on, I realize that I am truly his, bound to him not just by vows and promises, but by something that runs deeper, darker, and far more dangerous than anything I ever imagined.

CHAPTER 11
HIM

*S*he walked down the aisle like a sacrifice dressed as a queen.

And I—

I was already on my knees.

The moment she entered, the hall changed.

The flames stilled. The shadows leaned closer.

The magic at the heart of Cairndale stirred beneath my ribs like an ancient thing waking from slumber.

The gown was gold, but it could've been armor.

The rose in her hair bled black.

And her eyes... her eyes didn't look afraid.

She looked ready to *burn*.

I reached for her hand and felt the seal of our bond pulse beneath her skin. The ring had already marked her. The castle had accepted her.

But this—this vow—was different.

"I vow to give you everything your heart dares to desire..." I said.

And gods, I meant it.

Not because I was cursed to.

Because I *wanted* to.

She was not just a vessel. Not just a consort. She was *mine*. And I would devour kingdoms for her.

When she gave her vow in return, the magic cracked like thunder.

Our bond sealed.

Bloodless—but no less binding.

I led her from the hall in silence, through the ancient corridors, toward the chambers prepared for our night.

Roses on the floor.

Candlelight like falling stars.

Velvet shadows waiting to watch.

When I closed the doors behind us, the lock slid into place with a sound older than language.

She turned toward me.

And I came undone.

The gown didn't last long.

It tore like silk soaked in heat—my hands impatient, reverent, claiming.

She gasped, but didn't step back.

She stood bare before me, bold and trembling, and I felt something inside me *fracture*.

She wasn't a bride.

She was a flame sent to test me.

And I—

I wanted to burn.

I worshipped her with hands and tongue and teeth. I made her cry out. Made her beg. Made her arch against me like her body already knew mine.

And when I finally took her—when I pressed myself inside that perfect, wanting heat—something ancient surged between us. Not just lust.

Magic.

Old. Absolute. Consuming.

Every thrust was a vow.

Every moan a confession.

When I growled "You're mine," and she whimpered "Yours," the castle *sighed* in satisfaction.

We moved together like prophecy.

Rough. Beautiful. Endless.

I pushed her to the edge and pulled her over it, again and again, until she collapsed in my arms, wrecked and perfect and *mine*.

After, as the storm thundered outside and our bodies cooled in the heat of each other, I kissed her shoulder and asked, "Was that what you wanted?"

But what I didn't say was—

You were what I wanted.

And I never expected to get it.

Now she sleeps beside me.

And I lie awake.

Because I know what's coming.

The castle will test her.

The curse will try to claim her.

The power that binds us will demand its price.

And I'm no longer sure I'll let it take her.

CHAPTER 12
HER

T he bed is too large when I wake.

My body aches in ways both exquisite and unfamiliar—my thighs sore, my lips swollen, my skin a map of where he touched, kissed, claimed.

Cassian is gone.

His absence is a silence all its own, humming through the room like a storm that's passed but left its pressure behind. I shift under the silk sheets, each movement a reminder of the night before. My body remembers him even if the room pretends he was never here.

The air still smells like him. Earth and smoke and something darker, ancient, like crushed petals left too long in moonlight.

I press my face to the pillow, searching for the

warmth he left behind. There's a hollowness there now. The sheets cool. The silence louder.

Was I a bride... or just a willing offering?

I close my eyes and breathe.

My body pulses with the aftershocks of pleasure, with bruises that feel like marks of devotion. I remember the way he whispered to me—*You're mine.* The way he moved inside me like we were forged for this. The way he held me afterward, for a moment, like he needed me.

And still... he left.

I slide out of bed, wincing as my feet hit the cold stone floor. I ache everywhere. Between my legs, behind my ribs, in the hollow place just beneath my heart.

The room is bathed in pale morning light, all soft gold and faint shadow. It should feel peaceful. Instead, it feels like a lie.

I pull his discarded shirt from the floor and wrap it around myself. It dwarfs me, hanging off one shoulder, soaked in his scent. I press the collar to my lips and walk barefoot to the window.

Cairndale stretches out before me, veiled in mist. Spires rising like thorns. Forests curling against the castle's edges. A kingdom of secrets, shadows, and magic.

And now I am part of it.

Was it just sex?

Or am I being transformed?

My fingers touch the place where he kissed my throat. The place where he entered me. The place where I came apart and didn't care who I was anymore—only that I was his.

I shiver.

What if I want to belong to him... more than I want to belong to myself?

A memory rises—his hands in my hair, his voice low against my ear, the look in his eyes when I said "yours."

But doubt bleeds in.

Would he have held me if I hadn't said it? Would he have kissed my shoulder if I'd begged him not to stop? Or was that part of the ritual, too?

Did he mean any of it?

I step back from the window, returning to the bed, unsure whether I want to curl into the blankets or tear them all off and run.

And I am left there, standing alone in the wreckage of our union, wearing his shirt, aching in places I didn't know could ache—with this one unbearable truth carving itself into my ribs:

I had given him everything. My body. My vow. My soul.

CHAPTER 13

HER

L ife within the castle walls settles into an intoxicating rhythm. Every morning I wake in the opulent bed, the silk sheets a reminder of my gilded cage. Each night, I find myself both dreading and craving the darkness that falls, for it brings Cassian to me—my prince, my captor, my mysterious consort in this shadowed realm.

Tonight, as we lie together in the vastness of our bed, the moon casting silvery light through the window, the weight of all the unasked questions presses upon me. His name, though simple, had eluded me, lost in the whirl of magic, fear, and desire that defined our days. I turn to him, my head resting against his shoulder, the warmth of his skin a stark contrast to the cool air of the chamber.

In the shadow-draped silence of our chamber, I

find the courage to ask what has long lingered in my mind.

"Cassian," I begin, the name feeling both strange and fitting as it rolls off my tongue, a key unlocking doors long closed. "Why have I never asked your name before now?"

He turns to look at me, his eyes reflecting the moonlight, deep pools of shadow and light. "You needed to see who I was before you could know my name," he replies, his voice a low rumble that resonates in the silent room. "In the realm of the fae, names hold power, Ember. They are not just identifiers but bindings, spells woven into a single word that can hold sway over the very essence of a being."

I pause, absorbing the gravity of his words, the implications swirling like mist. "So, knowing your name..."

"It gives you a power over me, just as my knowing yours gives me power over you," he continues, a serious note underpinning his words. "But the essence of a person—their actions and choices—that is what truly defines them. That is the true measure of their spirit, beyond the simple syllables of a name."

I nod, the weight of this new knowledge settling over me like a cloak. "Cassian," I repeat, a little more confidently, letting the familiarity of it wash over me. It's a name that speaks of strength and mystery, of darkness bound with an allure I cannot escape, and now, of a shared vulnerability. "And in the fae realm, how are these powers, these bindings of names, usually handled?"

"With great care," he answers, his gaze steady. "Names are exchanged only when trust is absolute, for they can be used in oaths and bindings, in promises and curses. A name can be a weapon as much as a gift."

The room seems to grow colder with his words, the shadows deeper. "Have you ever regretted sharing your name?"

Cassian's smile is tinged with melancholy. "I have shared it but seldom, and only when the need was great or the bond was strong. Each time, it was a choice—a risk I deemed worthy." His hand reaches out, fingers tracing the line of my jaw gently. "As I deemed it worthy with you."

His touch, the sacredness of names among his kind, it all stirs a mixture of awe and fear within me. To think that he views our bond with such significance adds layers to our relationship I'm only beginning to comprehend.

"Then I will honor your name, Cassian, as a token of the trust between us," I say, my voice steady despite the racing of my heart. "And I will strive to be worthy of the power it grants me."

He pulls me closer, the distance between us closing as easily as the merging of shadows. "I believe you will, Ember," he murmurs, his breath warm against my skin. "For you have already shown yourself to be both brave and true."

In the quiet that follows, I lay my head against his chest, listening to the steady beat of his heart. The name—Cassian—echoes in my mind, a mantra that binds us deeper than any spell. In this moment, under the watchful gaze of the moon and the silent whispers of the ancient stones, I feel the power of the name, and of the man who bears it, weave its way into my soul, binding me to him with threads stronger than any magic the fae realm could conjure.

As DAYS BLEND within the walls of Cairndale, my understanding of my place here, by Cassian's side, deepens, twisting around my heart like the ivy that clings to the ancient stones of the castle. Each morning brings anticipation; each night, a dance with shadows that seduces more of my soul into the darkness.

Cassian is patient, methodical even, as he introduces me to the intricacies of the kingdom's governance. We spend hours in the vast library, its shelves heavy with tomes of arcane knowledge and dusty histories. "Understanding the land you will rule is crucial," Cassian tells me, handing me a leather-bound book whose pages whisper of ancient battles and dark pacts made under blood-red moons. The stories are compelling, filled with power struggles and betrayals, the magic of the land woven through every tale like a strong, unbreakable thread. I find myself lost in the narratives, each one shedding light on the complex tapestry of Cairndale's past and the role I am to play in its future.

During these lessons, Cassian watches me closely, his dark eyes missing nothing. He questions me, challenges my interpretations, and guides my insights, shaping my understanding not just of the kingdom's history, but of its present tensions and the delicate balance of power that holds it together. "Your role is not just to stand beside me," he explains one evening, as the sunset throws golden light across the library's floor. "But to stand with me. You must be as much a ruler as a consort, Ember."

The weight of his expectations is immense, but so is the thrill that comes with each new piece of knowledge, each secret unveiled. I feel myself growing, not just in power, but in confidence. Yet, with each step forward, I am reminded of the ring on my finger—the symbol of the bond that brought me here, a bond that is both gift and curse.

THE FOLLOWING MORNING, I was walking the castle grounds with Liana, the young maid who has become both my confidante and guide. As we pass through the vibrant gardens, her words paint a vivid picture of Cairndale—a land steeped in ancient magic and governed by traditions as old as the castle itself.

"Cairndale wasn't always like this," Liana explains, her voice soft, mindful of the ever-present walls that might carry our words farther than intended. "It used to be a place of light and laughter, much like the towns in Coral Cove. But as the magic grew stronger, it demanded more from its rulers and its people."

I listen, captivated by her knowledge, each detail helping me piece together the complex tapestry of my new home. "What changed?" I ask, genuinely curious about the transformation of such a place.

Before she could answer a gentle breeze stirs the air, carrying with it the distant sound of footsteps. I turn to see Cassian approaching, his presence commanding even from afar. The seriousness in his stride mirrors the gravity of our earlier conversation, reminding me that the stories of this land are more than mere tales—they are the very fabric of its existence.

"The magic became a part of us, part of Cairndale," Liana continues, her fingers pausing in their task of tending the roses. "It bound itself to the land, to the bloodline of the rulers. With each generation, the magic demanded more control, more sacrifices. That's why the rites you're undergoing are so crucial. They're not just about proving your worth— they're about binding you to the land, to its magic, to Cassian."

As Liana speaks, Cassian reaches us, his eyes flicking briefly over her before settling intently on me. There's a quiet authority in his gaze that stills the air between us.

"Thank you, Liana, that will be all for now," he says, his tone polite yet firm. Liana nods, casting me a sympathetic look before she departs, leaving a whisper of flowers in her wake.

Cassian's hand finds the small of my back. "Walk with me, Ember," he invites, his voice softer now that we are alone. We start along the path that winds back toward the castle, the stones cool and mossy beneath our feet.

Cassian watched the horizon where the garden

meets the shadowed woods. "The rites you are about to undergo, they are ancient, designed to deepen the bond and tie you to Cairndale, to its past and its future, and to me."

His admission hangs between us, heavy with implication. I stop walking, facing him. "Am I truly ready for this, Cassian? Is this what I want?"

He studies me, his expression unreadable. Then, reaching out, he lifts my chin gently with his fingers. "Are you asking if you're ready to accept the power and responsibility that comes with being my consort, or are you asking if your heart is ready to belong fully here, with me?"

Both questions unsettle me, but they also awaken a resolve within me. "I need to know," I say, my voice steady despite the whirlwind of emotions inside me. "Before I can answer either, I need to know what exactly I am agreeing to. What do these rites entail?"

Cassian's smile is tinged with both warmth and sorrow. "They are not merely formalities, Ember. They are enchantments, each one designed to weave your spirit more closely with the land and its lore. You will be tested, yes, but you will also be empowered. You will feel the magic of Cairndale flow through you, connect you to every leaf and stone and stream."

He pauses, his hand still holding my face. "And to me," he adds quietly. "You will be bound to me, not just by vows but by the very magic that sustains this land."

I search his face, looking for any hint of deceit or manipulation, but I find none. Only a solemn honesty that pushes me to make my choice. As the weight of his gaze and the future he offers anchors me to the spot, he whispers, a promise veiled in the encroaching dusk, "Tomorrow, under the ancient sky of Cairndale, you must decide, Ember. Will you flee from what you do not understand, or will you embrace the darkness with me, forever changing your fate?"

"I am ready," I finally say, my heart pounding with a mixture of fear and excitement. "I choose this path, Cassian, with you."

A relief seems to wash over him, softening the hard lines of his face. He pulls me into his arms, his embrace enveloping me in a sense of security and belonging.

"Then let us begin, my love," he whispers, pressing a kiss to my forehead. "Tonight, under the moon's watch, you will step into the circle of fire, and emerge as my queen, as much a part of this land as the magic itself."

As we walk back to the castle, my steps are

lighter, my decision made. The path ahead is fraught with challenges and darkness, but it is also filled with potential and power. And as I lean into Cassian, feeling the strength of his presence beside me, I realize that no matter how daunting the journey, I am no longer facing it alone. I am part of Cairndale, part of its magic, and irrevocably part of Cassian.

CHAPTER 14
HIM

S
he spoke my name for the first time last night.

Not as a title. Not as a question. But as a truth.

Cassian.

The moment it passed her lips, something ancient stirred in me. A lock turned. A door opened. And I knew I could never close it again.

She has my name now. Which means she has power over me. Real power—not just of body or bond, but of soul. The kind that could undo centuries of control if she so desired.

And I gave it to her willingly.

In the fae realm, that sort of trust is rare. Fools give their names. Lovers barter them like oaths.

Kings guard them like swords. But I... I gave mine because she had already taken everything else.

She took the edge off my rage.

She took the silence out of my nights.

She took the fear I had carved into myself to survive this crown—and softened it with one look.

She is Ember. And she is mine.

Not because I claimed her. But because she chose to stay.

I watched her while she slept this morning, curled among the silk sheets like something wild pretending to be tame. The moonlight still clung to her skin. Her lashes fluttered as if even her dreams refused to be still.

My queen.

She doesn't yet realize it, but she has already begun to change Cairndale.

The castle responds to her.

The shadows are quieter. The magic hums softer in the walls. Even the cursed soil that lines the southern gardens has begun to sprout again—tiny signs of life breaking through centuries of rot.

I should fear it.

I should fear *her*.

But I don't.

I ache.

There's a yearning in my bones I cannot name. It

isn't lust—though gods know I've hungered for her more than I've ever wanted anything. No, this is deeper. Older. Hungrier.

A need to protect her from the very throne she is being bound to.

A need to keep her from becoming what I had to become to survive this place.

I will not let Cairndale consume her the way it consumed me.

But I can't stop what comes next.

The rites are ancient. Binding. Brutal.

She will walk barefoot into the circle of fire. She will speak the names of the dead rulers who came before her. She will bleed into the earth. And if the land accepts her... she will rise more than a queen.

She will rise as Cairndale's soul.

And if it rejects her?

I don't let myself imagine that. I cannot. Because the truth is—I'm already bound to her. Not by ceremony. Not by magic. But by something far more dangerous:

Hope.

She is the first light I've allowed in since I buried my brothers. The first softness I've touched without fear of breaking it.

And tonight, she will walk willingly into the fire

—for me. For this kingdom. For a crown that neither of us asked for.

I must not show weakness. The court watches. The castle whispers. If they sense doubt, if they smell grief, they will strike.

So I bury it. As I always have.

Instead, I prepare the circle myself. I chalk the runes in blood and ash. I scatter bone-dust and lilies. I call the old magic from the roots of the keep and pray it remembers what mercy is.

Because tomorrow, I will bring her into that circle.

And I will ask the land to take her.

But the truth?

If it tries to take too much—

If it dares to break her—

I will burn this kingdom down with my own hands.

I have ruled in shadow for too long.

It is time the darkness met its match.

And her name is Ember.

CHAPTER 15
HER

The sky was a canvas of twilight, hues of deep blue fading into the soft blush of the evening star. The air was cool, a gentle breeze whispering secrets of the night as Cassian led me through the labyrinthine paths of the castle gardens. We moved silently, our footsteps a soft rustle against the gravel, until we reached a secluded part of the garden that I had never seen before—a place hidden from the casual gaze of the inhabitants of the castle.

As we entered the clearing, Cassian paused, turning to face me with a tender expression that softened the usual stern lines of his face. The fading light of the day cast shadows across his strong jaw line, lending him an otherworldly quality that took my breath away.

"Beautiful, isn't it?" he remarked, his hand gesturing expansively towards the ancient stone circle that lay before us. His voice was low, reverent, as if the sacredness of this place lent weight to every word.

I nodded, my eyes taking in the eerie beauty of the glowing runes. "It's like something out of a dream," I replied, the mystical atmosphere weaving its spell around me. The magic in the air was palpable, tingling against my skin like the soft caress of the wind.

Cassian stepped closer, his proximity sending a familiar rush of warmth through my body. "To me, this place is a reminder of the enduring power of our land, and now, of us." He reached out, brushing a stray lock of hair from my face with a gentleness that contrasted with the potent force I knew him to wield.

His touch sparked a heat that radiated through my veins, and I found myself leaning into him, drawn by the magnetic force of his presence. "I'm still amazed by how much there is to learn about this world—your world," I confessed, looking up into his eyes, which reflected the starlight and seemed to hold the depth of the night itself.

"And there is much I wish to show you, Ember," Cassian said, his hand moving to rest at the small of my back, pulling me closer. "Each rite, each piece of this land's history, every secret—it's now yours to share. But more than that, I want to share this journey with you, every step of the way."

The sincerity in his voice, the intensity of his gaze, it all made my heart flutter with something deeper, something that felt dangerously like love. "And I want to learn, with you," I murmured, my voice barely above a whisper.

Cassian smiled, a genuine, heart-stopping smile that made him look momentarily less like a prince of darkness and more like a man in love. "Then let us begin," he proposed, his voice carrying a new note of excitement. He led me by the hand to the center of the stone circle, his touch reassuring and firm.

As we stood together among the ancient monoliths, Cassian's demeanor shifted, the playful affection giving way to a more commanding presence befitting the ritual we were about to perform. "Tonight, you'll summon the Watcher of the West," he instructed, handing me the small, intricately carved talisman. "Focus your energy through this, and call to him. Remember, the strength of the summoning lies not just in the words or the talisman, but in the intent behind them."

I took the talisman, its surface cool and strangely smooth against my palm. "And what should my intent be?" I asked, seeking his guidance as I prepared to delve into the unknown.

Cassian's hand came to rest lightly on my shoulder, grounding me. "Your intent should be one of openness and strength. Show the Watcher that you are worthy of the knowledge and power he guards, that you are ready to embrace the duties of your new role alongside me."

His words bolstered my confidence, filling me with a determination to prove myself worthy not only to the Watcher but to Cassian and to the mystical land that was becoming my home.

With a deep breath, I raised the talisman, ready to begin the chant that Cassian had taught me, my heart pounding with the thrill of the magic we were about to invoke and the love that was surely, slowly binding us ever closer.

The ritual was not merely a test; it was an initiation, a step deeper into the mysteries of Cairndale and into my role beside Cassian. I stepped into the center of the stone circle, Cassian retreating to the edge, watching me with a daunting intensity that was somehow still comforting.

I closed my eyes, talisman before me, and began to chant the incantations Cassian taught me. The words felt strange on my tongue.

. . .

"O Watcher of the Western Skies,
    Guardian where the sun's light dies,
    Hear my call, from earth to stone,
    Across the veil, from flesh to bone.

By the twilight's last embrace,
    I summon thee to this hallowed place.
    Rise from shadow, rise from thrall,
    Watcher, guardian, heed my call.

Bind to me with wind and mist,
    Ancient keeper, by magic kissed.
    Reveal the secrets kept by night,
    Grant me sight beyond the light.

O Watcher, by these runes foretold,
    Join my circle, brave and bold.
    Stand with me, let our fates entwine,
    As I claim this right, this realm, as mine."

As I spoke, the breeze grew stronger, the whispering winds turning into a chorus that echoed my chants.
    Slowly, the air in the center of the circle began to

shimmer, like heat rising from stone on a hot day. A figure began to materialize, coalescing from the shadows and the light into an imposing form. The Watcher's appearance was otherworldly beauty and absolutely terrifying. His eyes were abyssal voids, profound and boundless, and when he gazed upon me, it felt as if he delved into the very core of my soul, uncovering secrets I had yet to whisper to myself. Fear spiked through me, a primal reaction to the supernatural presence before me, but Cassian's presence at the edge of the circle anchored me. I could feel his focus, his energy supporting me as I continued the incantations.

As I uttered the final word of the incantation, the Watcher's form seemed to shimmer with a newfound clarity. His head tilted slightly, an other-worldly gesture that suggested he was evaluating the sincerity and strength of my call. For a moment, the garden held its breath, the night air pregnant with anticipation. Then, with a slow, deliberate nod, he acknowledged my invocation.

No sooner had he consented than he began to chant in an ancient Fae tongue, his voice echoing like a melody spun from the very essence of twilight. The ground beneath my feet hummed with power as his words washed over me, enigmatic and resonant. As he chanted, an ethereal vibration began to course through me, starting at the soles of my feet and spiraling upwards, lifting me from the earth.

To my astonishment, I wasn't merely floating—I was ascending towards the sky, my body enveloped in a cascade of magical luminescence that painted the night with streaks of silver and blue. Cassian, his eyes wide with a mixture of awe and pride, stepped into the column of light that surrounded me. As he took my hand, his skin against mine sparked an intense, electrifying connection that felt as if the very magic of the land was weaving us together, binding us more deeply than any vow could.

Together, we soared above the castle, the land of Cairndale sprawling beneath us in a tapestry of shadow and starlight. Every second that passed brought us closer to an all-consuming ecstasy vibrating every inch of my body. It was as if the Watcher's magic was not only lifting us physically but was also elevating our very beings to a state of sublime unity.

We ascended higher and the magic intensified, sending orgasmic waves of pleasure through my body. Our joined hands became a conduit for this shared experience, each pulse of magical energy intertwining our fates intricately aligned with every beat of my heart.

The incantation reached its crescendo, the

Watcher's voice faded into the rustle of wind, and gently, like leaves falling back to the earth, we were lowered back to the sacred ground of the stone circle. The light that had enveloped us dimmed, settling into a soft lingering afterglow of the sun dipping below the horizon.

As our feet touched the ground, the intense vibrations of magic subsided, leaving us breathless and awestruck.

"You have done well," Cassian's said, a warmth flooded my body at his praise. His hand found its place on my back, a light touch that sent shivers down my spine.

The Watcher bowed slightly, his form beginning to fade, dissolving into the mist that had started to settle over the garden. "He has accepted your call," Cassian murmured, his breath warm against my ear in the cooling night air. "You are now recognized as a guardian of the West, a protector of Cairndale."

The thrill of the ritual's success mixed with the raw magic vibrating through my bones was exhilarating. As the last vestiges of the Watcher's presence disappeared, I turned to Cassian, finding solace in his approving smile.

Cassian led me back to the castle, and through the ornate doors, his hand at the small of my back sending shivers through me as we ascended the grand staircase to our secluded chambers. The echo of our footsteps mingled with the whisper of my gown against the ancient stone. As Cassian closed the doors behind us, the world outside faded away, leaving only the promise of forbidden pleasures.

His gaze, dark and full of unspoken desires, locked onto mine. "Tonight, we delve into the depths of our fantasies," he whispered, his voice a seductive promise that curled around my heart and tugged at its strings.

With a deft flick, the sash at my waist came undone, the fabric slipping from my shoulders to pool at my feet. His fingers traced the silhouette of my body, igniting trails of fire wherever they roamed. Every touch was a brand, every glance a conquest.

He guided me backward until the edge of the bed nudged my knees. His lips, fierce and demanding, found mine again, claiming me in a kiss that felt as though it could consume my very soul. He did not simply kiss; he devoured, coaxing out my deepest hungers and darkest wants.

Cassian's hands were both tender and commanding as they moved to bind my wrists with silk ropes, the knots snug yet gentle, a symbolic gesture of the trust between us. "Every tie that binds you, frees you a little more," he murmured, his breath warm against my ear as he secured each knot. His lips trailed a line of fire from my wrists down to my vulnerable neck, each kiss a spark that threatened to ignite the tinder of my restraint.

In the shadowed chamber, with only the flickering candles casting a soft glow, the air thick with the scent of jasmine and the distant echo of a storm outside, my world narrowed to the sensations Cassian evoked. Bound and blindfolded, the silk ties at my wrists and ankles taut against my skin, I was open to him—exposed and vulnerable in a way that thrilled and terrified me.

Cassian's hands, skilled and confident, traced the curves of my body, each touch igniting trails of fire. "You're at my mercy," his voice was a low murmur, a promise. His fingers danced across my skin, teasing and testing the limits of my restraint, drawing moans from deep within me.

I felt the air shift as he moved closer, the warmth of his breath a contrast to the cool air of the chamber. Then, his tongue found the core of my desire, my center, my aching pussy. His movements were deliberate, licking at my folds, drawing out each note of pleasure that spilled in sighs and gasps from my lips. The world fell away, leaving only the sensations he conjured—a tapestry of pleasure and pain, expertly woven by his hands.

As the tension built, spiraling tighter within me, Cassian paused, leaving me in absolute torture. I was so close to coming.

His voice a dark whisper against my ear. "I'm going to fill you first, to stretch and prepare you for me." The sound of his belt unbuckling was loud in the silent room, followed by the slick sound of a bottle being opened. Then, the pressure at my core as he guided a slick dildo inside me, slow and inexorable. The intrusion was a new edge of pleasure, stretching and filling me as Cassian moved the toy in and out, while he lapped at my clit, each thrust pushing me closer to the brink.

Feathers traced up along my sides, across my stomach and over my breasts, contrasting the sharper pleasure-pain of the nipple clamps he applied while still fucking me. Each one sending a jolt directly to the throbbing heat between my legs. The blend of soft and sharp, pleasure and pain, drove me higher, teetering on the edge of an abyss.

I was lost, floating in a sea of darkness when suddenly, the toy was removed, and I felt the heat of his body replace it. Cassian's hands gripped my hips, his presence commanding. "Now, me," he said, and I felt him—his thick cock—pressing deep into me. His movements were more intense than the toy's, full of heat and life and urgency.

Cassian's pace increased, relentless, driving both of us toward climax. "Let go," he commanded, and I did. The orgasm ripped through me, a scream torn from my lips, echoing through the castle. But he didn't stop, chasing his own release with a few more powerful thrusts until he too groaned, his body shuddering against mine, filling me.

After, he untied me slowly, each release of the binds punctuated with a kiss, a stroke, a whispered word of affection. Lying there, spent and wrapped in Cassian's arms, the candles burned low, casting long shadows across the stone walls. The outside world might as well have been a thousand miles away. In that room, we found a sacred space where only we existed, bound by whispers, shadows, and the immutable force of our destiny.

In the sanctity of our hidden world, under the watchful gaze of the moon through the casement window, I surrendered to the tempest, safe in the harbor of his arms. No ritual of the night was too sacred, no corner of my soul too dark as Cassian navigated the labyrinth of my desires, setting me free with every thread of restraint he unraveled.

CHAPTER 16
HIM

The garden is quiet tonight. Still.

It will not stay that way for long.

The moon rides high, its glow casting silver fire across the ancient stone circle where the earth remembers blood, sacrifice, and names once sung in the language of stars. I stand just outside the sacred threshold, watching Ember step into the center, talisman in hand.

She does not know what it cost to bring her here.

Not just through the slipper. Not just through the rites. But the deeper calling—the one older than kings or crowns. The one that burns at the base of my spine and whispers her name every time I close my eyes.

I called her soul to this place before she ever knew mine.

She raises the talisman, her voice clear despite the tremor in her bones. The summoning words fall from her lips, a cadence older than this kingdom.

It works.

It always works.

The wind answers first—restless, rising. The earth follows, humming beneath the stone. Then the shadows twist.

The Watcher comes.

He does not bow to me. Not anymore. I gave that right up when I refused to choose blood over balance. When I chose her.

He forms slowly, as if time itself must bend to accommodate his arrival. A towering figure robed in dusk and starlight, his face veiled in endless dark. But I feel his eyes settle on her. I feel them judge.

There is a moment where everything hangs—my kingdom, my magic, my heart—balanced on the edge of her voice.

Then she speaks the final line of the spell, and he nods.

Relief doesn't come. Not yet. Because I know what comes next.

I step forward, entering the circle, the ancient sigils burning beneath my boots. Magic climbs my spine like a thousand fevered hands. I take her hand,

and together we rise—suspended in a pillar of light born from a forgotten realm.

And gods help me, I feel everything.

The bond between us ignites. Not just a connection of magic, but of need. My flesh sings with it. Her soul calls mine like the sea calls the moon. And the Watcher's power flows through her, through me, until I feel the seams of my control strain.

She doesn't realize this is not just her test.

It's mine, too.

To see if I can withstand the pull of the power that pulses between us without breaking her. Without breaking myself.

I fail.

When we descend, the light is gone, but something darker pulses in its wake—raw magic threaded with lust and devotion. The Watcher fades, his task complete, leaving us stripped bare in more than body.

She looks at me like I am both god and storm.

I lead her back through the garden with trembling hands and a calm I no longer feel. The path to the castle is short, but every step is a war. I ache for her. Not just for her body, but for the way she looked at me when the magic surged. For the way she trusted me. For the way she made the ancient stones sing.

And when we reach the doors and I close them behind us, I don't speak.

There is nothing left to say.

Only the ritual that remains.

The taking. The tethering. The claiming.

She offers herself—bound and blindfolded—not out of obedience, but because she wants me to take control. To show her what it means to be mine.

I don't take it lightly.

I worship her with my hands and my mouth, with heat and ache and the slow unraveling of her restraint. She moans for me. She begs. And I give her everything—except mercy.

Because mercy is a lie, and I am too far gone for lies.

I stretch her with toys and words, with pain edged in pleasure until she trembles beneath me, open and trembling. Her cries undo me. Her silence undoes me more.

I take her then, not gently, not sweetly, but fully.

I fill her.

Mark her.

Lose myself inside her.

And when we both break apart, it is not just from pleasure—it is from the realization that there is no turning back.

She is mine.

And I am hers.

Bound by ancient magic, by spoken name, by whispered ache.

Later, when I untie her, I kiss every red mark, every bruise, every inch of skin that bore my hunger. I hold her close, her body limp in my arms, her breath slow and steady against my chest.

I whisper her name into the hollow of her throat.

She doesn't hear it.

But I say it anyway.

Because even now—even after all we've shared —I don't know what I've done.

I don't know if I've crowned her...

Or cursed her.

CHAPTER 17

HER

The sky bled into twilight, the horizon painted in strokes of deep blues and purples, the final whispers of daylight succumbing to the encroaching night. In our secluded chamber, high within the west tower of Cairndale Castle, Cassian stood silhouetted against the dwindling light, his form both menacing and magnificent. Tonight, like every night since our paths had fatefully crossed, promised explorations into the depths of desires darker and more consuming than the shadows that danced upon the ancient stone walls.

"Are you ready, my dear?" Cassian's voice was both a seduction and a challenge, his accent thickening in the dim light, echoing the dangerous allure of his homeland.

I nodded, my pulse quickening with a mixture of anticipation and fear. Tonight was not merely about physical exploration—it was about summoning the deeper, darker parts of our souls, parts I'd only dared whisper about in the dead of night.

With a deliberate slowness, Cassian approached, the soft sound of his footsteps a stark contrast to the thundering of my heart. In his hands, he carried the tools of our rite: whips whose leather tails gleamed under the flickering candlelight, wax candles poised to drip their searing kisses onto waiting flesh, and an ancient grimoire bound in shadows and whispers.

He set the items down with reverential care before turning to face me. His eyes, dark pools of infinite depth, held mine, promising both ecstasy and torment. "Trust is the essence of power," he murmured as he reached out to gently cup my face, his touch surprisingly tender.

My breath hitched as his fingers traced a path down my neck and along the curve of my shoulders, teasing the silk robe away from my skin. The robe fell in a whisper, leaving me bared to his gaze and the cool air of the chamber. His eyes flared with approval and something fiercer, something possessive. "Beautiful," he breathed, and the single word was laden with ownership.

Cassian guided me towards the center of the room where symbols and ancient texts lay inscribed upon the floor, their meanings as mysterious as they were powerful. With each step, my skin tingled, the very air charged with magic, thick with the scent of myrrh and something wild, untamed.

He directed me to stand within the circle, his hands deft at the ties that bound the silk ropes. "Every knot I tie, every line I draw, connects you deeper to the realm of shadows we call forth tonight," he explained, his voice low and hypnotic.

Bound and blindfolded, the darkness behind my closed lids seemed alive, shifting, a canvas for the play of sensations about to unfold. I felt the first drop of wax splatter against my chest, the pain sharp and sudden, yet it gave way to a heat that pooled deep within me, stoking the fire of my arousal.

Cassian's hands were on me then, his touch alternating between the cruel bite of the whip and the soothing balm of his palms. With each stroke, he painted stripes of fire across my breasts, bottom and thighs, the pain mingling with pleasure in a dance as old as time.

"Tonight, we transcend the physical," Cassian intoned, his voice weaving through the flickering candlelight. He began chanting in a language forgotten by all but the most devoted scholars of the dark arts. The room grew colder, the shadows deepening, coalescing into forms both mesmerizing and terrifying.

As the ritual reached its crescendo, the boundary between pleasure and pain blurred into insignificance. The chamber, our sacred arena of shadows and whispered chants, hummed with the potency of unleashed desires. Cassian, my dark conjuror, moved within that charged space as both master and part of the magic itself.

He entered me and it was both a claiming and a liberation, his size a stretch that filled me to the brink of both ecstasy and surrender. He leaned down, his breath hot against my ear, his movements calculated to stoke the fires of my arousal to white-hot intensity. "I'm going to put a baby inside you," he growled, each word laced with the promise of a future forged in the throes of our union. "You'll scream my name as you come, bearing the heir to my legacy."

His hands captured my breasts, his lips replacing the cool air with the heat of his mouth, biting and sucking on my nipples with a fervor that sent spikes of desire straight to the core of me. His words, dark and thrilling, unlocked something primal within me —an urge, a need that I hadn't known I possessed.

"Yes," I gasped out, the idea of carrying his child igniting a fierce and profound arousal. The thought of submission, of being so intimately bound to him through blood and bone, was unexpectedly powerful.

Cassian's thrusts grew more insistent, his length driving deep, each movement designed to claim, to imprint his essence within me. The world narrowed to the point of his possession, the overwhelming fullness, the exquisite friction. And when he promised out loud that he would make me scream his name, it wasn't a threat—it was a prophecy.

With a possessive growl, he bit down harder, his hips slamming into mine with a force that pushed me to the edge of climax. The room spun, the candles flickered, and the shadows danced to the rhythm of our coupling. My cry, when it came, was both a surrender and a claiming of its own, echoing around the chamber as he filled me with his release, his name a reverent invocation on my lips, "Cassian!"

But our ritual was far from over. With meticulous care, he shifted my still-quivering body, my legs held high in a pose that was both vulnerable and powerful, suspended between the realms of earth and ether. He watched me, his gaze intense as he noted the traces of his possession gleaming at my core.

"I won't let even a drop go to waste," he murmured, his tone worshipful as he descended between my thighs. His tongue found me, expert and knowing, drawing forth another climax that left me breathless and moaning. Between licks and praises, he whispered of old healers' tales, of how orgasm might aid conception. His words, his actions, all were designed to enhance the potency of the ritual, ensuring that every part of me was attuned to the magic we were weaving together.

As he pushed his seed back into me, his movements deliberate, ensuring his essence remained within, I was overwhelmed by the intensity and the profound connection. It was more than physical—it was spiritual, a merging not just of bodies but of fates.

When he finally allowed my legs to lower, the room steadied around us, the candles burning low. The darkness embraced us like a cloak, a protective barrier around the sanctity of what we had invoked. I lay there, spent and filled with a warmth that went beyond physical satisfaction, knowing I had crossed into uncharted territories of my own heart and soul under Cassian's guidance.

Cassian stood before me, his expression one of

fierce pride and tender conquest. He untied my bonds slowly, reverently, each rope leaving a trail of ghostly sensation on my skin.

"Yours," I whispered, the word a vow, a surrender, a claiming.

"Always," he replied, his voice a benediction that sealed my submission, wrapping it in the sacred darkness of our shared journey into the night.

As the candles burnt down to stubs, and the shadows retreated to the edges of the chamber, I realized the night had only just begun. And with Cassian by my side, I was ready to explore every dark corner of our desires.

Yet, with each day's passing, the ring on my finger—a plain, unassuming band of silver—feels heavier. It's a constant reminder of Coral Cove, of a life less complicated, less shadowed by the weight of ancient magic and dark desires. Sometimes, in the quiet moments just before dawn, I find myself fingering the band, contemplating what might happen if I were to take it off. Would I wake from this intoxicating dream? Would I even want to?

ONE EVENING, after a particularly intense encounter that leaves both my body and heart aching, Cassian sits beside me on the bed, his hand tracing idle patterns along my arm. "What are you thinking?" he asks, his voice a low rumble.

"I'm thinking about home," I admit, the words slipping out before I can stop them.

Cassian's eyes darken, a storm brewing in their depths. "And what of it? Do you wish to return?" His tone is careful, measured, but I hear the underlying edge.

"I don't know," I confess, feeling a pang of guilt. "Sometimes, yes. But then..." I pause, searching for the words. "But then, I look at you, I feel this," I gesture between us, "and I'm not so sure."

He watches me for a long moment, his gaze penetrating. "Ember, you are home. This—us—it's where you belong. Do you feel that?" His hand moves to my heart, pressing gently.

I look at him, at the man who has shown me realms of myself I never knew existed, who has guided me through darkness with a firm yet gentle hand. I realize then, with a clarity that startles me, that the thought of leaving him, of leaving this, hurts more than I anticipated.

"Yes," I whisper, the realization dawning like the first light of morning. "I feel it. I think... I think I might be in love with you, Cassian. With all of this."

His expression softens, something like victory and relief mingling in his smile. He leans in, his kiss sealing my confession, binding me to him with a bond forged not just in magic, but in something frighteningly akin to love.

"In love with the darkness," he murmurs against my lips, "and in love with me."

"Yes," I breathe, surrendering to the truth, to him. "In love with it all."

As we embrace, the ring on my finger—a simple circle of silver—feels lighter. The darkness no longer just something I am bound to, but something I choose, something I crave. With Cassian, in this castle of shadows, I have found a strange, twisted sort of peace, a belonging that is as terrifying as it is exhilarating. And as the dawn breaks, casting light on the tangled sheets, on the marks of our passion, I realize that I am irrevocably, undeniably his.

CHAPTER 18
HIM

S he stepped into the chamber like dusk given form—bare feet silent on cold stone, eyes burning with uncertainty and trust. I watched her from the shadows, where I belonged, where the weight of kingship and ancient magic coiled beneath my skin like a serpent waiting to strike.

Ember.

Mine.

She was radiant in her fear. In her want. In the flickering candlelight that painted her skin gold and made her body tremble with anticipation.

And tonight... tonight I would take her further.

Not just to the edge.

But through it.

"I summoned the darkness for you," I

murmured, stepping into her light, brushing the back of my fingers across the swell of her breast, already rising with each unsteady breath. "You said you were ready to carry my name... but what of my legacy?"

She nodded, but I didn't move.

Not yet.

"Words mean nothing in a land like this," I whispered, circling her slowly. "We speak in blood. In sweat. In the songs of the body that echo in the marrow. Do you understand what you asked for?"

"I do." Her voice trembled, but her spine held straight.

I smiled. Good.

"I'm going to break you open, Ember," I promised, kissing the nape of her neck. "To fill you with more than seed—magic, history, my power. You'll become a vessel. My queen. My altar."

She shivered.

I bound her carefully—silk at the wrists, tight enough to mark, loose enough to protect. The symbols on the floor pulsed, ancient fae magic responding to our intent. I traced each rune with the edge of a feather dipped in ash and clove oil, watching her skin react, rise, bloom beneath my touch.

"Tonight," I said as I tied the blindfold, "we don't pretend. We become."

The first drop of wax made her hiss.

Perfect.

Pain, yes—but power too. Pain that demanded surrender. That unlocked doors even pleasure could not reach.

I alternated the temperature—wax and ice, kisses and strikes of the whip. Her cries became music, her moans spells cast without a single word.

When I entered her, it was not just with flesh but with a purpose older than memory. Her body yielded like the land after rain—needy, fertile, sacred.

"I'll give you my child," I growled into her throat as I thrust deeper. "My heir. You'll carry my blood like a crown."

She screamed—my name, not in fear, not in pain, but in the voice of a goddess being made flesh.

Cassian.

My name on her lips was more binding than any vow.

But I wasn't done.

I watched her quiver, glistening and open, my seed spilling from her like moonlight. I wouldn't waste it.

I knelt.

And tasted her.

Tasted myself.

Tasted *us*.

With reverence and hunger, I whispered into her trembling thighs the words of conception rites passed down by my ancestors. Words that called the land to bless our union. Words that dared the old gods to watch us, to mark us, to choose us.

Then again, I filled her—deeper this time, slower. Worshipping. Worshipped.

When she finally collapsed into me, her body wrecked, her spirit raw and glowing, I untied her slowly. Tenderly. As one would unwrap a relic.

She looked at me with something fragile behind the lust.

Not just submission.

Not just desire.

Love.

And it terrified me.

Because I felt it too.

As I whispered "Always," and kissed the bruises I'd left, I knew what I had done wasn't just ritual—it was surrender. Mine as much as hers.

She was no longer just a woman bound to the throne of Cairndale.

She was the throne itself.

And I would kneel, conquer, and rule her for all the dark nights of our immortal reign.

CHAPTER 19

HER

The night air is crisp, a blanket of stars scattered across the sky like a tapestry woven by the gods themselves. Cassian and I stand on the balcony of the castle, the stone cool beneath our feet, the realm of Cairndale spread out before us—a kingdom caught between shadow and starlight, magic pulsing through its very veins.

Cassian's gaze is fixed on the horizon, his profile etched against the night like a sculpture of a forgotten king. When he finally speaks, his voice is soft, caring the weight of centuries. "Ember, the time has come for you to choose," he begins, turning to face me. His eyes, usually a storm of dark and light, hold a seriousness that roots me in place.

"You can return to your old life and the world outside this castle you knew before," he said, his tone steady and serious. He paused, his gaze meeting mine, searching for a reaction. "But if you choose this path, you must leave behind everything you have learned here, everything you have felt. Your memories of me, of us, of all that has transpired in Cairndale, will be erased."

The weight of his words hung heavy in the cool night air. My heart raced as I realized this was the moment to reveal my own truth, a secret I had kept closely guarded since my arrival. Taking a deep breath to steady my nerves, I reached for his hand, feeling the familiar warmth of his skin against mine.

"Cassian, there's something I haven't told you," I began, my voice barely above a whisper. "I'm not originally from this world. I came here through a ring, a magical ring from Coral Cove. It brought me to Cairndale, to you."

His expression remained unchanged, his eyes still fixed on mine with an intensity that made me momentarily breathless. For a second, I worried how he would react, but then, almost without missing a beat, he nodded slowly.

"I know, Ember," he replied softly, squeezing my hand gently as if to offer reassurance. His calm acceptance of my revelation surprised me, and I found myself blinking back a mix of relief and confusion. "Thank you for trusting me with your truth. It changes nothing of my feelings for you, but it's important that you know you always have a choice."

The moonlight cast shadows across his brow. "If you decide to return to Coral Cove, you can. The ring that brought you here holds the power to take you back to your world. But you must understand, if you leave, the magic of the ring will also erase all memory of Cairndale and of what you and I have shared. You would wake up in your old life as if none of this had ever happened."

His words, spoken so calmly carried such finality. It made my heart ache with the gravity of the choice before me. The thought of forgetting him, our nights filled with magic and passion, the deep connection we forged—how could I ever choose to erase that from my mind?

Cassian's voice brought me back from my spiraling thoughts. "I want you to stay, Ember, not because you feel trapped or because you have no other choice, but because you choose this life, this love, with me, with your whole heart."

As he spoke, his gaze never wavered from mine, his eyes shining with hope and something akin to fear—the fear of losing me to a life I might decide to return to. In that moment, I realized how much he truly cared, how deeply he feared the possibility of my departure.

The choice was mine, and mine alone. Stay and embrace the life we could build together, with all its unknowns and magic, or return to a past that now seemed like a distant dream, devoid of the color and life Cassian had brought into my world. The decision lay heavy on my shoulders, a pivotal moment that would define the course of my very existence.

The thought of forgetting him, forgetting the rush of flying through the dark woods, the thrill of summoning ancient spirits, and the intoxicating power of standing by his side sends a pang of loss through me. To return to a life devoid of magic, of him, feels like a sentence to a shadow life, devoid of color.

"Or," he continues, his hand reaching out to cup my cheek, drawing me back from the precipice of my thoughts, "you can stay. Stay and rule beside me, embrace the pleasures and the perils of this land, and of its king."

The choice hangs between us, heavy as the moon above.

Cassian's touch is gentle, a stark contrast to the enormity of his offer. "Tell me about the others," I whisper, the question that has haunted my thoughts since I first heard the whispers in the town. "The others who came before me, with rings like mine. Did you... did they..."

"No," he cuts in, his expression hardening at the thought. "No, Ember. I did not harm them. They simply·chose to return to their lives, as you might now. They wore rings too—much the same as yours. They are a passage, a bridge, back to the worlds from which they came. Their memories of Cairndale wiped clean, as if they had woken from a dream."

I reel from the revelation, my heart a mix of relief and sorrow. "And you've never spoken of this because..."

"Because I am bound by the magic that governs those rings, bound not to interfere once they have made their choice to leave. They returned home. As you can, if you wish it," he explains, his voice a murmur that blends with the night wind.

I lean into him, my head resting against his chest, feeling the steady beat of his heart. Life before Cassian, before Cairndale, flashes before my eyes— the mundane job I loathed, the superficial relationships, the utter lack of magic. It all seems like a dream now, a pale shadow of the vivid, vibrant reality I've lived here. Here, I have felt alive, truly alive, for the first time.

"How can I choose to leave?" I ask softly, the answer already forming in my heart. "How can I forget all this, forget you?"

"You don't have to," he says, his arms encircling me, pulling me closer. "Stay with me, Ember. Let us face whatever comes, together."

The choice, once so daunting, now seems clear. I think of the deep, dark love I've found with Cassian. I think of the color he has brought to my world, the shades and hues of Cairndale that have painted over the drab palette of my previous life.

"I will stay," I whisper, my voice resolute. "I choose this life, with you."

A smile, both triumphant and tender, spreads across Cassian's face. "Then let it be so," he declares, and the magic of the moment seals my fate.

We stand together, rulers of a land as wild and mysterious as our future. And as I gaze into the night, into the depths of the kingdom I now call home, I realize that I am no longer torn. I am whole, bound not just by magic or fate, but by a choice made freely and wholly.

The stars witness my decision, twinkling their silent approval as I embrace my new life, my heart beating in time with the land itself, with Cassian. And as we turn to enter the castle, hand in hand, the night whispers of tales yet to be told, of magic yet to be explored. And I step forward, not just as Ember, but as the queen of Cairndale, ready to weave my own story into the fabric of this enchanted realm.

CHAPTER 20
HIM

S he stands beside me, cloaked in moonlight, and I know the gods are watching.

Not the kind that wear crowns or demand sacrifice. The older ones—the ones who stitch fate with bone needles, who lace destiny through the skin of mortals and monsters alike. They bear witness now, as Ember faces the threshold that has swallowed so many before her.

I should speak first. I always do when we reach moments like this. But the words burn in my throat, caught somewhere between hope and desperation. I am ancient. A creature of ritual. Yet tonight, I am simply a man hoping he will not be left behind.

"Ember," I say, forcing the calm into my voice, smoothing out the jagged edges of longing. "The time has come for you to choose."

I turn to her fully, the stars behind her, haloing her in silver.

"You may return," I say. "To the life you had before, the world you once called home. The ring you wear holds the magic to take you back."

My hand flexes at my side. I do not reach for her. Not yet.

"But," I continue, voice soft as stone breaking, "if you choose that path, your memories will be erased. You will forget Cairndale. Forget me. It will be as if none of this—none of *us*—ever happened."

The wind shifts, brushing her hair across her face. She doesn't flinch. She's too still. Too quiet.

It terrifies me.

Before I can fill the silence with reassurances, she speaks.

"Cassian," she whispers, "there's something I haven't told you."

She tells me about the ring—about Coral Cove, about how she fell into this world through magic older than language. Her voice is raw, threaded with guilt, fear, wonder.

I listen. I do not interrupt. I knew, of course. I have always known.

"I know," I say when she finishes. My hand finds hers, anchoring her trembling fingers in my steadier grip. "I've always known."

Her eyes widen, but she doesn't pull away.

"I was waiting for you to tell me," I add. "Because that trust, that choice to share truth—that is more powerful than any spell."

The moonlight strikes her ring then, a silver flash that gleams like a blade. I want to rip it from her hand. Cast it into the sea. But I don't.

Because if I cage her, I lose her.

So I give her the truth. All of it.

"There were others," I say, because she deserves that. "Not many. A few, scattered across time and space. The ring finds them. Or they find it."

She asks the question I've feared since she first stepped through the portal: "Did they... did you...?"

"No." My voice sharpens with the force of my certainty. "I did not harm them. I did not love them. They came. They chose. They left."

I look into her eyes and let her see what none of the others ever did: grief, honest and raw.

"They never remembered me. The ring sees to that. It erases me completely."

And that is the deepest cruelty. Not that they leave—but that they wake with empty hands, while mine remain stained with the memory of what might have been.

"But you," I say, cupping her cheek with reverence, "you have not left yet."

I let her lean into my touch. Let her breathe.

"Stay," I whisper. "Not because I ask it. Because *you* want it. Because this—*us*—is worth remembering."

The silence that follows is unbearable. My heart pounds like war drums beneath my ribs. She could still say no. She could still choose to forget. And I would let her.

Even if it ruins me.

But then—

"I will stay," she says, voice steady. Final.

I do not fall to my knees. But I want to.

Instead, I pull her into my arms and hold her as though I can graft her into my very soul. As though by holding her tightly enough, I can rewrite fate.

"Then let it be so," I whisper into her hair.

The magic stirs around us. Not the sharp, ancient power of spells or spirits. Something deeper. Older. The magic of *choice*, of two lives twining not by force, but by willing hands.

Ember has chosen Cairndale.

She has chosen *me*.

And as I lead her back inside, our fingers laced and sure, I know this is not the end of the story. Not even close.

This is the beginning of a reign born of blood and shadow. Of love tempered in fire. Of a kingdom ruled not just by power—but by devotion.

And I will guard her choice for the rest of my immortal life.

Even if the stars forget her name, I never will.

Also by Jax Wilder

Coral Cove Series

Sleighed by Love

Harvesting Love

Dawning Desire

Knead You Now

Love Rewound

Perfect Lover Spell

Haunted by Her

Red, White, and Ravished

Tarot Fantasies Series

The Devil's Temptations

Strength of the Beast

Hanged Passions

Six of Cups

Death's Embrace

Queen of Pentacles

Seven of Pentacles

Ace of Wands

Three of Swords

Lovers In The Veil

<u>Two of Swords</u>

Seven of Wands

Coastal Cupid Series

HeartBound Souls

Witches of Coral Cove

From Hell With Love

Fae Ring Series

Alice and Her Mad Hatters

Bound By The Glass Slipper

Stand Alone Titles

Pride and Prejudice and Witches

LORELAI HAMILTON

Encyclopedia of Divination

Encyclopedia of Cryptids

Encyclopedia of Faeries

Tarot Tales and Magic Spells

Teenage Tarot

Arcane In Verse

The Eclectic Witch's Grimoire

Teenage Witch's Grimoire

Find Your Bliss

Tarot Reflection Journal

Tarot Refection Journal Coloring The Tarot

Dream Journal

MIRANDA LEVI

From A Youth A Fountain Did Flow

The Sea Withdrew

A Tear In Time

Mo(ther) Na(ture)

In Orion's Hands

JACKSON ANHALT

From The 911 Files

ISLA WATTS

A Fairy Bad Day

Surprise! You're a Vampire

Gorgeous, Gorgeous, Gorgons

Mork The Handsome Orc

Adopted By Werewolves

Bite Me If You Can

That's The Spirit!

ROSE DAWSON'S BOOK JOURNALS

My Time With The Fairies

Enchanted Escapades

Enchanted Escapades

Dewey Decimal Diaries

Siren's Songbook

Pride and Prejudice

Bibliophile's Bounty

Book of Books Journal

Pages & Passages Reading Journal

Bookworm's Companion Reading Journal & Tracker

ILLIANA BARRET

**Prompted: 2,339 Romance Prompts: A Writer's
Essential Resource**

**Prompted 1,700 Fantasy Prompts: A Writer's Essential
Resource**

Prompted 1,605 Science Fiction Writing Prompts: A Writer's Essential Resource

Prompted 1,902 Horror Writing Prompts : A Writer's Essential Resource

Prompted 1,290 Mystery Writing Prompts : A Writer's Essential Resource

Prompted 1,582 Children's Book Writing Prompts: A Writer's Essential Resource

Prompted: 2,265 Historical Fiction Writing Prompts : A Writer's Essential Resource

Prompted 1,500 Steampunk Writing Prompts

Prompted: 1,600 Dystopian Prompts: A Writer's Essential Resource

About the Author

Jax Wilder is a passionate romance author hailing from a charming small town nestled in the picturesque Pacific Northwest. With a heart full of love and an unyielding belief in the power of happily ever afters, Jax weaves enchanting tales of love and connection that leave readers captivated.

Jax's novels are a reflection of her commitment to celebrating the magic of love, and her characters' journeys mirror the warmth and happiness she has found in her own life. Join her on the enchanting journey of love, passion, and enduring connection through her heartfelt romance novels.

www.ingramcontent.com/pod-product-compliance
Lightning Source LLC
Chambersburg PA
CBHW051954170626
46808CB00007B/2621